SILVER KNIGHT

25 Remarkable Years of Championship Indiana Basketball

Written by Bob Hammel
Photographs by Rich Clarkson

With additional photography from the staff of the Herald-Times

The Herald-Times, Inc.   Bloomington, Indiana   *A Rich Clarkson Book*

The Herald-Times, Inc., 1900 South Walnut Street, Bloomington, Ind. 47403

Printed in the United States of America
First Printing, February 1997
10 9 8 7 6 5 4 3 2 1

Library of Congress Cataloging-in-Publication Data
Bob Hammel, Rich Clarkson
    Silver Knight: 25 Remarkable Years of Championship Indiana Basketball
    ISBN 1-890073-02-__
    1. Bob Knight, 1940–   2. Indiana Hoosiers (basketball team)
    3. Basketball coaches, Indiana (biographic)

Book Design by Thomas C. Ema & Robin H. Ridley, Ema Design Inc., Denver, Colorado
Printed by Shepard Poorman Communications Corporation, Indianapolis, Indiana

Marketing by Sidelines Sports

C O N T E N T S

When they met in a hotel room in Houston in March 1971 – 30-year-old Army coach Bob Knight and the Indiana University search committee athletic director Bill Orwig headed – chances are no one was thinking of history.

Indiana needed a basketball coach. Knight, after six seasons at Army that subsequent results grade as remarkable, felt he wanted to move. Indiana's 17-7 season had ended in a player rebellion that Orwig felt demanded a disciplinarian.

All those things dovetailed nicely.

But Orwig, who died at 86 in 1995, always remembered one other thing about those early meetings with Bob Knight.

"After he had come to Bloomington and we had talked everything over and were sitting in my living room, I asked him, 'Why did you want to come to Indiana?'

"He said, 'I can win there.'

"Isn't that a great answer? I like a guy who says 'I can win.'"

Orwig checked Knight out with some Eastern friends.

"They said he was a little tempestuous, but that has never bothered me," Orwig said. "We needed someone who was a strong disciplinarian. We knew that Bob certainly would give us that.

"And we knew with Assembly Hall opening that year, we had to have a pretty good group of people in there. We felt a winner would bring them in, and we felt Bob could win.

"The interview (with Knight, by the committee) was just tremendous. He was so well prepared.

"I remember that we each had a rating sheet, and when we finished, Bob was No. 1 on every sheet."

A quarter-century later, there is a special college athletic era to study. The Bob Knight program has indeed won. But, high as the standards and accomplishments are there, the program's best testimonial is its people – the long, continuing line of exceptional young guys who wore INDIANA across their chest and, with their coach that they came to play for, achieved a border-to-border bonding that, game night after game night, year after year, made their captivated state proud. The roster of Knight lettermen from Indiana alone gives representation to 34 towns and communities, 47 high schools, from every section of the state. And the lists will grow with Luke Recker from DeKalb, already signed on for 1997-98, and Jarrad Odle, who as an Oak Hill junior announced IU plans.

Back at the dawning of all this, Knight's arrival in the state in late March 1971, the change was major for both him and Indiana fans, not to mention the players

From his early days in Orrville on, Bob Knight was always pointed toward a coaching career.

he inherited who had been recruited to – and signed on for – another system and coaching philosophy.

"The challenge of coaching at this level was why I came here," Knight said. "I came for about half of what I was getting at Army. Money never really bothered me in this context. I always figured it could be made. If you do a good job, you're going to be in demand to do things."

Knight's Silver Anniversary season at Indiana was his 31st as a head coach. He had won 102 games and lost 50 at Army, from 1966 through 1971, when recruits knew their future was not the NBA but Vietnam. Knight's Army team had strong backing. Major General Ray Murphy, the athletic director who gave the 24-year-old Knight the Army job, said, "I've never seen a period in my lifetime at the academy when the student body was so buoyed by a team. You talk about *esprit* – the basketball team brought it on, but it was fortunately the corps that was pushing the basketball team. I thought that was a good thing, and I haven't seen it since. Magnificent."

The campus, the student body and the fan following were bigger and the victory rate picked up with his move to Indiana. Knight is one of just seven coaches who in 30 or more years as a major-college head coach won games at a .700 or better rate. He is in line to be the seventh major-college coach ever to win 700 or more games, the ninth or 10th to win 600 at one school. He is one of three coaches to win three or more NCAA championships, the only one of that group to add an Olympic championship.

"I don't know whether Bob could have had as much success at more than one or two other places in the country – North Carolina, maybe, but not many,"

6

(Far right) Captain Quinn Buckner checks out a real seat of power, in the Oval Office at the White House.

(Right) President Gerald Ford, a one-time Michigan football MVP, was a gracious host to Bob Knight and the Indiana team that beat his alma mater for the 1976 national championship.

Orwig said. "And I'm sure some of those other fellows we talked to would have been winners.

"But I don't think anybody would have ever built the program the way Bob has built it. It's hard to improve on a Hall of Famer."

That – induction into the Basketball Hall of Fame in Springfield, Mass. – came for Knight in 1991, at age 50.

His trip there started considerably earlier.

He grew up in Orrville, in northeastern Ohio, population then about 5,000. "My mom was a schoolteacher. I started going to the library when I was 7 years old. They had kind of a yellowish, gold series of American biographies – George Washington, Alexander Hamilton, Thomas Jefferson. And then I got into those books by John R. Tunis. And I read all of Clair Bee's books (a 23-book fiction series that had as its main character high school athlete Chip Hilton).

"Till I got into basketball a little bit, I just thought Clair Bee was a writer of boys' books. I had no idea he was a coach."

Knight played four years at Orrville, well enough that the new, young coach at Ohio State, Fred Taylor, included him in his first big recruiting class at Ohio State, by at least one criterion – future Hall of Fame membership – maybe the best recruiting class in basketball history. Jerry Lucas, John Havlicek and Knight from that class and the coach who recruited them all are in the Hall at Springfield.

The Buckeyes were 78-6 in that group's three varsity years, 40-2 in league play – winning three straight Big Ten championships and never losing a league game till that year's title was clinched. They made it to the NCAA championship game each year, beating California for the 1960 title and losing to Cincinnati in both 1961 and '62.

Knight minored in history at Ohio State. There was a time he thought he would go to law school, maybe as a graduate assistant on John Wooden's staff at UCLA. But, though his railroadman father couldn't understand why anyone would go to college to learn to coach, that always was son Bob's career intention. Not that he disagreed with his father's main point. "I thought physical education was a waste of time," he said. "I wished I had majored in English – still to coach."

After a year as an assistant coach at Cuyahoga Falls, Ohio, High School, happenstance got him an invitation from Army coach George Hunter to volunteer for the draft and serve two years at West Point as an assistant coach. He volunteered, and Hunter was fired. Hunter's successor, Taylor "Tates" Locke, picked up the commitment. Two years later, Locke left to coach at Miami of Ohio. Bob Knight, 24, became one of the youngest head coaches ever in major college basketball.

He has, at times, subjected himself to the same questions anyone with a long career in one field has: Would he have been better off being a lawyer, or perhaps something else?

"I don't know. It has been a really good life for me. Where else am I going to be financially independent? I could have quit several years ago, if I had wanted to,

The books, the packages, the
daily stacks of mail accumulate
too quickly for Bob Knight's
desktop space to handle.

and been able to live comfortably the rest of my life.

"Had I not made as much money as I have, enabling me to do the things I want to do – the fishing, the hunting, the golf, whatever – I honestly can't tell you I'd have stayed in coaching. I've been offered a lot more money to do other things.

"But it worked out great for me. I could send my kids to school – Tim went to Stanford and Patrick (who played for him at Indiana) could have gone wherever he wanted to go."

Even he wonders why he has stayed with it beyond all professional goals, beyond all financial needs. He wonders, but he also knows the answer.

"There's the challenge of the game – the machinations of the offense, and the positioning of the defense, and playing from one game to another. I love the game of basketball. I just think it's the greatest game of all.

"The clock has taken something away from me. The 3-point shot has taken something away from me. I'm not as good a coach as I was before the clock and the 3-point shot. When we got ahead before the clock, we didn't lose. It was more of a coaches' game then than it is now."

Fans, he's quite aware, like the game better now.

"The 3-point shot is popular because people want to see home runs. They can understand that. They can see a kid get open (in pursuit of an old-fashioned 2-point basket), but they don't see the kid working for position, the ball reversed – bang, it goes inside and the kid lays it in. All they see is, 'Oh, he made an easy shot.' They don't see what has taken place to get the ball into that position to score. But they can see the kid hitting the

(Far left) Winter means more than just basketball for avid bird hunter Bob Knight.

(Left) Fishing, too, gets its due in Knight's life, and his crowded office.

3-point shot, and they get excited about it. I don't like the 3-point shot. I don't think the shot is good enough to get an extra point. There are scores in basketball that are more difficult to come by than the 3-point shot."

An intent of the rule creating the 3-point shot line was to de-clog the game. "If you've got good 3-point shooters, sure, it opens things. But I would be an advocate of the international lane, the trapezoidal lane, to get the wrestling further away from the basket. The further they remove the postman from the basket, the less wrestling you're going to have between offense and defense.

"And the better you are, the quicker you are. That's an axiom in basketball you can't escape." The game has had other changes as well. "At one time, defense guarded the basket. Now, defense pressures the ball. That's a big difference."

Knight lists as his personal coaching heroes Taylor, Bee, Pete Newell, Red Auerbach and Joe Lapchick. Taylor and Newell have been careerlong confidants and close friends for Knight. Bee, Auerbach and Lapchick each did some coaching where Knight has no desire to go: professional basketball.

Auerbach's Hall of Fame berth came strictly from NBA dominance. He is on Knight's Most Admired list "because I watched the way he motivated people and the way he got people to play. I just liked him. I liked his presence. He was a combative, competitive coach."

Bee, who won more than 80 percent of his games at Long Island University before some career-closing years in the young NBA, "was a brilliant guy. We talked about using people. Although he was a great advocate of zone defense in a team concept, he thought kids had to learn to play man-to-man defense before they could do anything else — that that was the basis for everything."

Lapchick had outstanding success at St. John's, but he also openly used the NBA to build up a bank account that enabled him to go back to college coaching. He counseled the young Army coach to consider doing the same thing some day. Knight listened but, when the offers came, had no problem walking away from them to stay at Indiana. A key requirement for a pro coach, he feels, is "the fortitude to accept all the bull that he's going to have to accept. He's going to have guys making $2 million who can't play. That would always bother me: I'm looking at this guy making $2 million and he can't crush a grape."

Lapchick counseled him in other ways, too.

"He just knew how to coach, how to get kids to play hard. He asked me once, 'Is it important to you that you are liked? Because if it is, you can't coach.' That was his premise, because you're going to make too many decisions based on what is going to upset somebody."

Such a possibility never has concerned college coach Bob Knight. He finds enough concerns in the coaching role itself.

"Rarely does a kid have the same role in college that he had in high school. The kid we get is obviously the best player on his team — probably the best player in the city, maybe in the state. So he has been pampered.

(Below) If only the walls could talk – they do, in Bob Knight's coaching quarters.

(Right) The lockerroom approach is the same for Knight's 26th Indiana team as for his first.

BY YOUR OWN SOUL LEARN TO LIVE
AND IF MAN THWART YOU PAY NO HEED
IF MAN HATE YOU HAVE NO CARE
SING YOUR SONG, DREAM YOUR DREAM
PRAY YOUR PRAYER
BY YOUR SOUL LEARN TO LIVE

14

"We get all of these guys who, probably when they come here, envision themselves being as good as Calbert Cheaney." Cheaney was the College Player of the Year in 1993. That year, he also became the leading scorer in Big Ten history, his 2,613 career points still the best ever in a league that always has had great scorers.

"They don't realize Cheaney was able to move to that level, and I think we really elevated Cheaney – (two-time consensus All-America Steve) Alford not so much but Cheaney we moved to another level, the same as we did with Mike Woodson.

"We've always had good shooters here."

In those first 25 Knight years at Indiana, the Hoosiers led the Big Ten in shooting 10 times, in free-throw percentage 9 times, in the 11 years of 3-point shooting 5 times – leading the nation in 3-point percentage in 1987, '89 and '94.

"Think about this for a second," he said. "Our system, had Woodson not gotten hurt (missing seven weeks after back surgery his senior year, 1979-80), would have produced three of the six leading scorers in the history of the Big Ten. Obviously our emphasis is on the team as a whole, but as we cut that up into roles, there is a role for a really good shooter and a scorer – perhaps more

(Right) Indiana's 1987 national champions were honored on the White House lawn by both President Ronald Reagan and Vice President George Bush.

(Far right) The ever-active, ever-demonstrating, ever-teaching hands of Bob Knight.

so here than anywhere else.

"When I was a senior in high school, I scored 45 points in a scrimmage game and led the scrimmage in rebounds and assists, too. What I got back after that (from the coach) was 'That's too many points for one guy to score.' Our team really deteriorated because of an exaggerated sense of a team concept. I honestly believe that's one reason why kids who have played for me who could score have scored."

In December 1995, the best of Knight's teams – two of the best in college basketball history – gathered for a reunion. It was the 20th-anniversary year of the unbeaten national champions, but neither Knight nor most Indiana basketball fans can think of that year without the 31-1 season that preceded it. So, seniors of 1975, including Knight's first IU recruit, Steve Green, also were part of the program.

They heard from their coach what they and those years, with their impact on all the subsequent years, have meant to the man with the hard-bitten demeanor.

On Senior Day 1976, Knight recalled, "I made the comment 'Take a good look at these five, because I don't think you will ever see their equal again.' And I can say that easily here tonight, 20 years later – I can say it about the players who represented both teams, the two graduating classes and the underclassmen who came along behind these players. They were a rarity, a real exception.

"You only maybe get that one great pitch to hit, and these kids all hit it well. They took advantage of the opportunities they had. Some went on to have really good careers in the NBA, but everyone went way beyond basketball. Each one has been very, very successful in whatever he has chosen to go into.

"That, to me, is the enduring quality of what athletic participation is all about – players who were able to win championships and have been able then to take what they've learned in winning those championships to do the same thing with their lives.

"They've all talked about what a privilege it was to play at Indiana, to be on teams like they played on, how much they gained from it and enjoyed about it. Yet, the privilege that they felt in playing at Indiana is absolutely nothing compared to the pleasure and the privilege I feel in having coached these players.

"There were times I'm sure they wondered really how much I liked them. And there were times, I'm sure, one or two of them might have said, 'The SOB is never satisfied.'

"Well, to a degree, that's true. I'm really tough to satisfy. As far as basketball was concerned, on that night in March when we beat Michigan in Philadelphia for the national championship, from a basketball standpoint, then I was satisfied.

"From a personal standpoint, though, as I've watched each of them grow – there, too, I'm satisfied. And my being satisfied with them as people is a hell of a lot more rewarding to me than just being satisfied with them as basketball players."

Indiana 90   Kentucky 89   Double Overtime

Freedom Hall   Louisville, Kentucky

December 11, 1971

Going in, it looked like a game for history. Looking back a quarter-century later, it seems a game for history. And on the Saturday night it was played in legend-loaded Freedom Hall, 17,269 people who watched it and rode its wild swings up and down and rooted with the passion this series brings out went off into the night saying what usually isn't said about anticipated games.

It *was* a game for history.

It was Adolph Rupp in his last year at Kentucky against Bob Knight in his first at Indiana.

No.		Height	Class	G-S	Pts.
44	Joby Wright*	6-8	Sr.	25-25	19.9
42	John Ritter	6-5	Jr.	25-25	14.0
32	Steve Downing	6-8	Jr.	25-25	17.5
20	Frank Wilson	6-3	Jr.	24-23	7.4
22	Bootsie White	5-8	Jr.	24-21	6.6
24	Dave Shepherd	5-10	So.	11-3	5.8
54	Kim Pemberton	6-3	Jr.	16-2	3.3
33	Jerry Memering	6-7	Jr.	23-1	2.3
43	Rick Ford	6-4	Sr.	21-0	1.9
23	Steve Heiniger	5-10	So.	12-0	0.8

* All-Big Ten

The new coach, the new arena: the Bob Knight/Assembly Hall era begins in Bloomington.

It went double overtime, and Knight's team won by a Rupplike score, 90-89. In the final seconds, Kentucky's Bobby McCowan put up two shots, and the rebound from the second was rolling out of bounds when the gun sounded.

Knight's team won because it had a warrior named Steve Downing, whose week-old knee injury made his playing status so doubtful going into the game that Knight had contingency plans. "We'll start Steve," Knight said. "If he can't go hard, we'll have to take him out. We have to attack Kentucky in the middle."

Downing stayed in. He played all 50 minutes. He scored 47 points. He had 25 rebounds.

"Why, I couldn't even have conceived it," Rupp said afterward, the totality of Downing's achievements jumping off the statistics sheet he held in his hand.

"Boy, he's going to make a fuss in the Big Ten," Rupp said.

Knight had turned 31 just seven weeks before the

(Top) The trucks are still unloading at brand new Assembly Hall as Indiana's 31-year-old new coach starts to work.

(Bottom) In an exhibition game with Australia that was the first game ever played in Assembly Hall, Knight talks at a timeout to Steve Downing (32), Bootsie White (22), Jerry Memering (33), John Ritter and Kim Pemberton, while reserves, managers and assistant coaches listen.

game. This was his fourth game at Indiana, his 156th as a head coach, his 106th victory. Rupp had turned 70 a hundred days earlier. This was his 1,042nd game at Kentucky, his 184th loss.

Downing was the game's dominant player throughout. Indiana jumped out 5-1 and 13-6; by then, Downing already had eight points and his Kentucky matchup, center Jim Andrews, had two fouls.

Rupp countered with a 1-3-1 zone to protect Andrews and swarm Downing. In little more than 10 minutes, the Wildcats – running and firing and getting early bombing from guard Ronnie Lyons – scored 35 points to go up 41-30.

The Lyons toll was part of the price Knight paid in setting up a defense against Kentucky's scoring leader, Andrews. Normally, Downing would have been playing Knight's denial defense, trying to shut off Kentucky's access to Andrews. But not on this night, not with Downing's sore left knee. "We knew we couldn't have Steve out in front of Andrews and still expect him to do the job offensively," Knight said. "We kept Steve

behind Andrews and we told the others to help out all they could by sagging back in. It cost us some baskets outside, but I felt it was better having them shoot out there than Andrews in close."

Bootsie White was the Indiana guard covering Lyons. "At first, I was more conscious of sagging in on Andrews and figured I'd let Lyons have those long shots," White said. "But he hit a couple, so I just said to myself, 'Okay, he's hot. I'll have to move out on him.'

"But he hit some more."

After a timeout, Indiana scored 10 straight to trail 45-43 at half. "That stretch was a key point in the game," Knight said. "We didn't have to play catch-up ball the last half."

Downing had 23 points and 12 rebounds that first half.

The second half was played at a pace more favorable to Knight. On offense, he kept the ball in White's hands. He wanted to cut Downing's trips up and down the court as much as he could. "I told them we were holding the ball," Knight said, "but if (White) saw an opening clear to the basket, he could go – provided he could either get the layup or drop the ball off to Downing."

At 0:34, White put Indiana up 74-72 with a free throw, then stole the ball back (0:23). With 13 seconds left, White lost the ball to a double-team in center court and Stan Key's shot at 0:06 caused overtime.

Downing obviously was tired. Knight just as obviously didn't consider pulling him. "Did Calumet Farms take Seabiscuit out when he got to the home-stretch?" he answered a postgame questioner.

Lyons hadn't hit a field goal the entire second half. In the first overtime, he hit four in a row, each edging the Wildcats out front. Each time, Indiana caught up, John Ritter's free throw at 0:53 bringing the 82-82 tie that carried into the second overtime.

Downing still was dominating. He scored twice inside, but Kentucky stayed even (86-86). Downing's free throw at 3:06 put Indiana up for good.

The Hoosiers got the ball back and White drove to a layup and an 89-86 lead with 2:26 left. Downing's 25th

Steve Downing set the Assembly Hall rebounding record that still stands (26) in the building's official opener against Ball State, but Kerry Hughes (54) and Wisconsin dropped an overtime surprise on the Hoosiers at The Hall.

Senior Joby Wright twists for inside points in the Hoosiers' first Big Ten victory for their new coach, over Michigan State.

rebound got the ball back one more time, but Kentucky had some moxie left. When White broke to get open for a pass, McCowan moved into his path. They collided; a whistle blew. "I saw him out of the corner of my eye," White said, "and then he jumped out in front of me. I thought it would be on him."

It was on White, his fifth. McCowan and Indiana's Jerry Memering matched free throws (90-87), Andrews scored for Kentucky (90-89), and Wilson's one-and-one with 0:29 left bounced out.

So did those last two McCowan shots, and the two teams ended 50 frantic minutes one point apart.

Rupp allowed that the Hoosiers were aggressive. "We thought there was a lot that wasn't called. They may play a little rougher in the Big Ten.

"But I'll tell you, if you can't play with the big boys you might as well not play. If you can't whip the bully on the street you should go home and play with dolls."

He wouldn't let up on Andrews, who that year went on to score more than 600 points, average 21½ points a game and make first-team all-SEC for a co-championship team. This night, he had 22 points and 13

rebounds, but in Rupp's mind were the many ways Downing victimized him. "We told Jim to take a step out," Rupp said, "but he didn't. He didn't then, he never has, and he never will."

Knight's mind was on his own man. "I've never seen a college basketball player play a better ballgame than Steve Downing did tonight," he said.

"I guess that's his opinion," Downing said. "And I guess I thought I played pretty well, too.

"But I had a bad game on defense.

"I kept wondering if (the knee) would go out on me, but it never really got bad. It was more a case of being stiff than being sore. I was trying to protect it and got myself off-balance a couple of times.

"I wanted to win bad."

These Hoosiers were to crash the polls' Top 10 in pre-conference play, then lose their first four league games. They won nine of their last 10 games and made the school's first appearance in the NIT. It was a brief one. Princeton, the first team young Bob Knight met as a 25-year-old head coach at Army, eliminated the Hoosiers at Madison Square Garden, 68-60.

1971 – 1972		
17-8; Big Ten 9-5, Third		
Ball State	W	84-77
Miami, Ohio	W	65-50
Kansas	W	59-56
Kentucky [1]	**W	90-89
at Ohio	L	70-79
Notre Dame	W	94-29
at Butler	W	85-74
Brigham Young [2]	W	61-50
Old Dominion [2]	W	88-86
at No. Illinois	L	71-85
at Minnesota	L	51-52
Wisconsin	*L	64-66
at Ohio State	L	74-80
at Michigan State	L	73-83
Michigan State	W	83-69
Minnesota	W	61-42
at Wisconsin	*W	84-76
Iowa	W	86-79
at Illinois	W	90-71
at Purdue	L	69-70
Michigan	W	79-75
Ohio State	W	65-57
at Northwestern	W	72-67
Purdue	W	62-48
N I T		
Princeton [3]	L	60-68

* Overtime
** Double Overtime
[1] at Louisville
[2] Old Dominion Tournament, Norfolk, Virginia
[3] at Madison Square Garden, New York

21

Indiana 77   Purdue 72

Assembly Hall

March 10, 1973

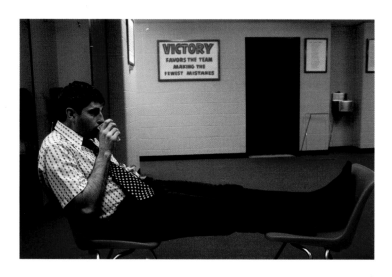

After a tight game, even two chairs can feel like a sofa.

The pieces were still fitting together in the Bob Knight building project at Indiana when the Hoosiers took the floor for their final game of the season, against Purdue.

The Hoosiers had seemed out of the Big Ten race after an 82-75 loss at Minnesota dropped them into

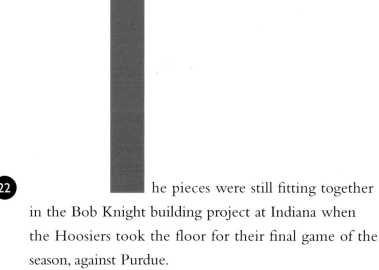

No.		Height	Class	G-S	Pts.
34	Steve Green	6-7	So.	28-26	10.1
42	John Ritter	6-5	Sr.	28-27	14.7
32	Steve Downing*	6-8	Sr.	28-28	20.1
21	Quinn Buckner	6-3	Fr.	28-27	10.8
45	Jim Crews	6-5	Fr.	28-22	5.3
31	John Laskowski	6-5	So.	28-1	10.3
30	John Kamstra	6-1	So.	13-0	3.9
55	Tom Abernethy	6-6	Fr.	18-2	2.2
22	Trent Smock	6-5	Fr.	16-0	1.4
41	Craig Morris	6-4	Fr.	11-0	1.7
33	Jerry Memering	6-7	Sr.	14-0	1.3
35	Don Noort	6-8	Fr.	12-0	1.3
20	Frank Wilson	6-3	Sr.	13-5	0.9
24	Steve Ahlfeld	6-0	So.	14-0	0.9
25	Doug Allen	6-5	So.	10-0	0.2
22	Bootsie White	5-8	Sr.	4-0	0.0

All-Big Ten, Big Ten MVP, All-Final Four

third place three weeks earlier. They did their job the rest of the way, but the help they needed to get back into the race came early in the final week of the season. Iowa – beaten 80-64 at Iowa City by the Hoosiers two days earlier – shocked reigning champion and league leader Minnesota on the Gophers' court, 79-77, on Kevin Kunnert's 3-point play with four seconds to go.

That sent 3,000 IU students into the streets and on to a late-night celebration at the school's old football stadium. It also sent the Hoosiers into the Purdue game sharing the lead with Minnesota, which was to close out its season later in the day at 1-12 Northwestern. Conferences could send only one team to the NCAA tournament then, and arrangements were made for a tie-breaker between Indiana and Minnesota on Monday night at Champaign to pick that NCAA team.

It wasn't needed. Indiana beat Purdue, 77-72, and Northwestern stunned Minnesota, 79-74. Indiana was the clear-cut champion, headed for what would

(Top) Against a backdrop of the peppermint-striped warmup pants that came in with him in 1971 and became a Bob Knight-Indiana trademark, Knight talks to the team that first took him to the Final Four.

(Bottom) There's no question about where the eyes are focused during a preparation meeting.

Indiana's Red Steppers –
a leg up on a longtime run.

be a Final Four berth.

Knight had played down the stretch with three rookie starters – sophomore forward Steve Green and, in the first year of a new freshman-eligibility rule, freshman guards Quinn Buckner and Jim Crews. Another rookie, sophomore John Laskowski, had emerged as the team's "Super-Sub." Laskowski's South Bend St. Joseph's High teammate, freshman Tom Abernethy, had come on well in the Big Ten season. Another freshman, John Kamstra, was moving into prominence until a torn Achilles tendon ended his year in January.

But the Hoosiers' leaders were clear: seniors Steve Downing, who was to be the first of Knight's eight Big Ten Most Valuable Player award recipients, and John Ritter, an undersized forward (6-5) with exceptional shooting skills.

They were holdovers from a freshman class Knight's predecessor, Lou Watson, had brought to campus in the fall of 1969. The group's headliner was George McGinnis, top-rated high school player in the land that year. He played Watson's last year and turned professional.

Downing teamed with McGinnis on one of Indiana's all-time best state champions, unbeaten Indianapolis Washington. Those two, Ritter (from Goshen), Jerry Memering (from Vincennes, which also reached the State Final Four unbeaten) and Bootsie White (Hammond Tech) were Indiana All-Stars. The recruiting group also included guard Frank Wilson of Bluffton, a pre-med student who started at guard with White for most of Knight's first IU season.

In this second Knight season, White, playing little, left the team and school. Memering's role was reduced; Wilson's was cut even more. The great freshman class that was the fruit of Knight's first full recruiting year at Indiana caused the changes.

The Hoosiers shot out to a 6-0 Big Ten start and drew their first national attention of the Knight era, but the loss at Minnesota Feb. 17 was their third in a row on the road and the bloom seemed off. When the Hoosiers had a shaky 55-53 lead late in their next-last home game of the year against Wisconsin, Green went diving over the out-of-bounds line trying to make a steal. The crowd of 15,000 responded with a soft patter of applause. Knight rose and thrust a fist in the air toward the fans, obviously demanding more enthusiasm for Green's effort. After the Hoosiers scraped through, 57-55, Knight's postgame press conference was hot and brief:

"I think it is an absolute crying shame that 15,000 people can sit there on their dead asses at a ball game and a coach has to get up to get somebody to cheer for a bunch of kids who have given these people the basketball that these kids have."

The crowd at The Hall when Purdue came in for the final Saturday of the year was anything but dead.

Sophomore Steve Green was
a key rookie starter for
Knight's first Big Ten champions.

Purdue jumped out 8-0. Freshman Crews hit twice in a row over Purdue's 3-2 zone and Indiana went to halftime up 41-35. "The guys that hurt us inside were the same ones that hurt us (in a 70-69 Purdue win) at our place – Downing and Green," Purdue's first-year coach, Fred Schaus, said. "But Crews (14 points, his season high) killed us outside."

In a matchup of standout freshman guards, Purdue's Bruce Parkinson had all the better of it over Buckner, until the end. Parkinson's 3-point play, then steal and basket pulled Purdue within 71-66 with a minute left, when Buckner twice broke Purdue's press for baskets that completed the knockout.

Schaus went to the Indiana lockerroom to congratulate the new champions. Once back to his own dressing area, a box score of the game in his hands, Schaus was less amiable.

"Indiana had four less baskets but they got 24 free-throw attempts to our 8," Schaus read. "That's the difference – the free-throw attempts.

"I think it's a shame that two teams work as hard as these two and key calls by the officials not necessarily make the outcome of the game but influence it.

"But I'm not saying that cost us the game. We lost to a good basketball team."

Knight noted the game "just kept bouncing back and forth, which indicates to me there were a lot of pretty good kids out there."

There also was a pretty good crowd out there, he acknowledged with a tease. "I felt the crowd responded pretty well…to the Wisconsin game."

In the game's final seconds, court announcer Chuck Crabb advised the fans to stay seated after the game for a presentation. Crabb himself had been advised just seconds before. The start of what was to be a Knight-IU-Assembly Hall tradition, "Senior Day,"

wasn't advertised at all in advance.

After the Purdue players had cleared the floor, Knight, with his own team still on-court behind him, expressed his thanks to the crowd and to Watson, "the guy who brought these men to Indiana."

Knight then made that team's four seniors the first to be brought to mid-court microphones to say goodbyes to the home crowd.

They weren't ready with the speeches that later seniors prepared. Wilson, who was to go on to a medical career, gave the seniors their valedictory.

"Four years ago," he said, "we all came here with one goal: to win a Big Ten championship."

Back in the lockerroom, Ritter said, "Frank was right – the thing we all felt when we came here was that we wanted to put Indiana back on top." Indiana had finished last in the Big Ten three of their four high school years and in the year they sat out as freshmen. "This," Ritter said, "was a game we all wanted to win *real* bad."

In NCAA tournament play at Nashville, the freshman guards whipped the renowned Marquette press, and Downing one more time led the way past Kentucky, to the Final Four at St. Louis. There, although Downing outscored Player of the Year Bill Walton, 26-14, UCLA outlasted the Hoosiers, 70-59 – a 22-point UCLA lead down to 3 when a late-game block-charge decision averted Walton's fifth foul and led to Downing's.

But the new Indiana program, its young coach, and his recruits had made their splash.

Steve Downing, Bob Knight's first Big Ten MVP, led the young Hoosiers to the Final Four and there outscored Bill Walton, 26-14.

1972 – 1973		
22-6; Big Ten 11-3, Champion		
Harvard	W	97-76
at Kansas	W	72-55
Kentucky	W	64-58
at Notre Dame	W	69-67
Ohio	W	89-68
at South Carolina	L	85-88
Houston [1]	W	75-72
Texas-El Paso [1]	L	65-74
Ball State	W	94-71
at Wisconsin	W	78-64
Miami, Ohio	W	80-68
Ohio State	W	81-67
Minnesota	W	83-71
at Michigan State	W	97-89
at Michigan	W	79-73
Northwestern	W	83-65
at Ohio State	L	69-70
at Purdue	L	69-72
Illinois	W	87-66
at Minnesota	L	75-82
Michigan State	W	75-65
Wisconsin	W	57-55
at Iowa	W	80-64
Purdue	W	77-72
N C A A		
Marquette [2]	W	75-69
Kentucky [2]	W	72-65
UCLA [3]	L	59-70
Providence [3]	W	97-79

[1] *Sun Bowl, El Paso, Texas*
[2] *at Nashville, Tennessee*
[3] *at St. Louis*

25

Indiana 82 Northwestern 53
McGaw Hall Evanston, Illinois
January 26, 1974

The last major moment in the emergence of Bob Knight basketball at Indiana came somewhere in late January 1974. Maybe in an Iowa City hotel room.

The Hoosiers had come back rather well from their surprise Big Ten championship and more surprising drive to the Final Four in 1972-73. Graduation had taken their two best players, Steve Downing and John Ritter, leaving a team without a senior. Downing's spot, center, was so wide open freshman Kent Benson moved into it almost on opening day of practice. Still, the year before had made such Knight-believers across the land that the Hoosiers began the year ranked among the elite. A pre-season poll listed Indiana No. 3 in the land, behind only UCLA and North Carolina State. It was that situation that spawned a classic Knight-ism. Taking questions after a November talk to a Bloomington service club, Knight was asked about that No. 3 ranking. Remember, Knight cautioned, such polls are the cumulative wisdom of sportswriters, whose lot got a quick description: "All of us learn to write in the second grade, but most of us go on to other things."

Early losses to Notre Dame and Oregon State, then a 73-71 defeat at Michigan opening the Big Ten season, dropped the Hoosiers from the national picture. Their stature with their own followers dipped, too. The afternoon of Jan. 19 – after watching Notre Dame come from down 70-59 to score the last 12 points and end UCLA's 88-game winning streak – Knight was well into the taping of his pregame interview with first-year IU Network announcer Don Fischer when Fischer asked: "Coach, this team is 10-3 but there is a general feeling that it isn't playing very well. How would you respond to that?"

The answer was: hotly. Knight had been stretched out in his hotel-room bed during the taping. He started an answer, bit it off quickly, sprang out of the bed, and declared the interview over. "It's the first time I ever

No.		Height	Class	G-S	Pts.
34	Steve Green*	6-7	Jr.	28-28	16.7
42	Scott May	6-7	So.	28-27	12.5
54	Kent Benson	6-10	Fr.	27-25	9.3
21	Quinn Buckner*	6-3	So.	28-27	8.2
24	Steve Ahlfeld	6-0	Jr.	22-12	3.1
31	John Laskowski	6-5	Jr.	28-3	12.5
33	Tom Abernethy	6-7	So.	28-1	5.7
20	Bob Wilkerson	6-6	So.	28-4	3.6
45	Jim Crews	6-5	So.	22-9	2.8
30	John Kamstra	6-1	Jr.	14-0	1.7
22	Trent Smock	6-5	So.	18-2	1.6
43	Don Noort	6-8	So.	18-1	1.6
23	Craig Morris	6-4	So.	14-1	1.6
25	Doug Allen	6-6	Jr.	12-0	1.1

Green: All-Big Ten; Buckner: All-Big Ten

Cheerleaders sail high and happy at Assembly Hall, but for Bob Knight, between trainer Bob Young (left) and assistant coach Dave Bliss with sophomore Jim Crews, coaching life is ever-intense.

1973 – 1974		
23-5; Big Ten 12-2, Co-champion		
Citadel	W	74-55
Kansas	W	72-59
Kentucky [1]	W	77-68
Notre Dame	L	67-73
at Ball State	W	87-62
South Carolina	W	84-71
Brigham Young [2]	W	96-52
Oregon State [2]	L	48-61
Oregon [2]	W	58-47
at Michigan	L	71-73
at Miami, Ohio	W	71-58
Wisconsin	W	52-51
Northwestern	W	72-67
at Iowa	W	55-51
at Northwestern	W	82-53
Iowa	W	85-50
Illinois	W	107-67
at Wisconsin	W	81-63
Michigan	W	93-81
at Illinois	W	101-83
at Minnesota	W	73-55
Michigan State	W	91-85
at Ohio State	L	79-85
Purdue	W	80-79
Michigan [3]	L	67-75
C	C	A
Tennessee [4]	W	73-71
Toledo [4]	*W	73-72
Southern Cal [4]	W	85-60

*Overtime
[1] *at Louisville*
[2] *Far West Classic, Portland, Oregon*
[3] *Playoff, Champaign, Illinois*
[4] *at St. Louis*

Steve Green, Bob Knight's first Indiana recruit, heads for the goal.

heard sheets crackle," Fischer recalls now with a grin.

But Knight also knew his young team *was* struggling. Winning most of the time, but struggling. That night at old Iowa Fieldhouse, Knight watched that continue. With 6:46 left, Iowa led 48-42. A rebound basket by sub Tom Abernethy put the Hoosiers ahead for good in a 55-51 victory. So the Hoosiers were 11-3, and 3-1 in the Big Ten. And struggling.

In the 2½ seasons of Bob Knight-Indiana basketball up to then, the emphasis on protecting the basketball was typified by a rule on outlet passes: 15 feet, maximum. At practice the Monday after the Iowa game, that rule was eased, though 20 years later, Knight said, "I still like15 feet – I still don't like long outlet passes." But he has operated ever since that post-Iowa weekend with a faster pace, the focus on getting the ball out and down the court, for a fast-break basket if possible, quick entry into the offense if not.

The new attack's emergence came at the end of that

week at Northwestern. The Wildcats were 6-8 and confident going into the game. Two weeks earlier at Assembly Hall, Northwestern had the ball with 27 seconds to go, down 68-67, but all-time NU scoring leader Billy McKinney was called for stepping on the sideline – bumped there by burly Quinn Buckner, Wildcats coach Tex Winter contended. Indiana used the reprieve to win, 72-67.

That was an atypically high score. In nine games through the 55-51 victory at Iowa, the Hoosiers had averaged just 60 points a game. Starting with an 82-53 breakout in the rematch with NU at Evanston, the same Hoosier team averaged 87 points a game. Unsuspecting Northwestern was burned for six fast-break layups, and the Hoosiers introduced something that was to become nationally fashionable a basketball generation later with the 3-point shot. When the layup wasn't there on breakouts, shooters Steve Green, Scott May and John Laskowski fanned out to the sides – at 3-point range now – and converted passes into quick jump shots that would have been forbidden before. Green was 12-for-15 that night, May 4-for-4 and Laskowski 3-for-5, a combined 19-for-24.

It was a game that Knight had to watch with gritted teeth. The Hoosiers had 30 turnovers in their upbeat debut, "the most we've had in a long, long time," he said. "But we also got some points from things other than our (half-court) offense."

Laskowski by then had become the Hoosiers' "Super-Sub," logging as much playing time as any starter. Sophomore Bobby Wilkerson also was emerging as a more and more frequent contributor from the bench. Sophomore May was starting but problems with footwork confined him to just those four shots he hit.

The Hoosiers went on to win 12 in a row, eight of those after the change of pace. Maybe the Game of the Year came in the regular-season finale, an 80-79 victory over Purdue at Assembly Hall. The Boilermakers led 74-64 with 9½ minutes left, 79-78 when Laskowski stepped to the free-throw line with eight seconds to go. Laskowski hit both shots for a second straight 20-point performance off the bench, classmate Green blocked Mike Steele's shot, and the Hoosiers were Big Ten co-champions – with the Michigan team that won the league's only NCAA berth, 75-67, in a playoff with Indiana at Champaign.

In that epochal game at Northwestern, freshman center Benson was 2-for-4 on free throws. In his first 14 college games, he hadn't hit a free throw, a quick gauge of his involvement. Three weeks after Northwestern, he had a 20-point, 15-rebound game as Indiana vaulted into the Big Ten lead with a 93-81 victory over Michigan. He ended that freshman year by being named MVP when Indiana, rebounding from its playoff disappointment, won the first Conference Commissioners Assn. tournament at St. Louis.

May, whose constant traveling violations contributed liberally to the 30 turnovers at Northwestern, worked extra hours, day after day, with assistant coach Dave Bliss to get big-time basketball footwork down. Two weeks later, May was 11-for-12 for 22 points as the newly Hurrying Hoosiers unloaded 107-67 on Illinois. A year later, he was a consensus All-American.

And the greatest team in IU basketball's grand history was on its way.

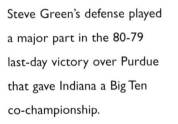
Steve Green's defense played a major part in the 80-79 last-day victory over Purdue that gave Indiana a Big Ten co-championship.

Indiana 83   Purdue 82

Mackey Arena   West Lafayette, Indiana

February 22, 1975

T he best of games, the worst of games.

"I don't know how you would find a better basketball game than the one played today," Indiana coach Bob Knight said. His team won, 83–82. Losing coach Fred Schaus of Purdue agreed: "If you didn't like this game, you don't like the game of basketball."

(Left) With Boilermakers all around (Bruce Parkinson, 20; Wayne Walls, 40), John Laskowski slips a pass to Kent Benson.

(Right) All-America forward Scott May led Indiana to a 104-71 victory over Purdue at Assembly Hall, but the rematch at Mackey Arena was not nearly so joyful for May or Hoosier fans.

No.		Height	Class	G-S	Pts.
42	Scott May*	6-7	Jr.	30-27	16.3
34	Steve Green*	6-7	Sr.	31-31	16.6
54	Kent Benson*	6-10	So.	32-32	15.0
21	Quinn Buckner*	6-3	Jr.	32-32	11.8
20	Bob Wilkerson	6-6	Jr.	32-32	7.2
31	John Laskowski	6-6	Sr.	28-6	9.5
33	Tom Abernethy	6-7	Jr.	32-0	4.2
22	Wayne Radford	6-3	Fr.	26-0	3.1
40	Jim Wisman	6-2	Fr.	23-0	2.2
43	Don Noort	6-8	Jr.	27-0	2.0
32	Mark Haymore	6-8	Fr.	23-0	1.7
45	Jim Crews	6-5	Jr.	26-0	1.4
24	Steve Ahlfeld	6-0	Sr.	28-0	1.1
30	John Kamstra	6-1	Sr.	24-0	0.9
25	Doug Allen	6-6	Sr.	22-0	0.5

* May: All-America, Big Ten MVP;
May, Green, Buckner, Benson: All-Big Ten.

The victory clinched a clear-cut Big Ten championship for the Hoosiers, just the fifth of those in school history.

And it was Indiana's blackest day of the year. The team Knight considers his best ever probably lost the national championship during this game.

Late in the splendidly played first half, Indiana forward Scott May set himself to go after a rebound at Purdue's end. "I've looked at the films," May said. "I was looking

Seniors John Laskowski and Steve Green went out with a powerhouse.

at the ball in the air, and (Purdue freshman forward Wayne Walls) kinda slid over to my left side. I had my arms (extended), ready to jump, and Walls' arm was on top of mine. When the ball hit the back of the rim, I jumped for the rebound. He didn't jump, so my arm hit his.

"That's the only time I can see where it could have happened."

In the heat of the game, he remembers no pain, but numbness developed in the arm. With 2:24 to go in the half, May went to Knight on the sidelines and said, "Coach, I can't squeeze my hand." Knight looked at May's left arm and told trainer Bob Young, "Take Scott to the lockerroom."

"I think he knew it was broken," May said.

Young's examination didn't take long. May couldn't turn the arm over. "When I did try," he said, "the whole wrist just collapsed. I could feel the bones cracking and touching each other. You could actually hear it. There was no question in my mind." X-rays at a hospital confirmed that the largest bone in May's muscular left forearm, the radial, had been cracked in two by an unnoticed, painless blow.

The game went on. Indiana, which had stormed through its first 14 Big Ten games by an unprecedented average winning margin of 27 points, led 50-46 at halftime. Senior Steve Green hadn't played in the first Indiana-Purdue game because of flu. Indiana won that day, 104-71, "Super-Sub" John Laskowski stepping in as the starter and scoring 13 points. The Hoosiers' splendid

play that day with Laskowski filling in no doubt figured in to Knight's later decision on replacing May.

But Green's flu problem wasn't solved easily. Over a 10-game stretch, he scored just 77 points. The week of the rematch with Purdue, Knight commented that Green for the first time since the problem developed looked strong and fit.

At Purdue, he was both of those. And sharp. He was 9-for-9 in scoring 20 first-half points, and Indiana led 50-46. He finished the day 13-for-15, virtually every shot dead center. The last of those, glanced off the backboard from about 15 feet out on the side, broke an 80-80 tie with two minutes left. Eight times in a row up to then, Purdue had pulled even and Indiana had scored to edge in front. This time, center Kent Benson came up with an interception and the Hoosiers, with 1:41 to go, went into a stall. At 0:29, Green slipped loose for a layup, but a foul averted the basket and he missed one of the free throws. Walls scored quickly for Purdue to make the score 83-82. Buckner broke Purdue's press to bring the ball up the sideline into frontcourt, but when he pulled up on the drive, his foot slipped. Walls, three inches taller than Buckner, dived in to force a midcourt jump ball (at 0:11), then controlled the tip.

Purdue tried to jam the ball inside to center John Garrett, but Wilkerson's kick deflected the pass and stopped the clock at 0:05. Purdue quarterback Bruce Parkinson took the in-bounds pass and tried to spin away from the long-armed Wilkerson, but the ball popped

Kent Benson's play around the basket helped the Hoosiers to a key overtime win at Kansas and continued through an All-Big Ten year for the sophomore center.

free, Buckner grabbed it out of the air and lofted a high, clock-killing pass toward the Indiana end.

May had returned in time to watch the last 25 seconds. "That was enough," he said. "That was tough."

It was Indiana's first win ever at Mackey Arena. It made the Hoosiers 15-0 and eliminated runnersup Purdue and Michigan (9-5 each). It protected the No. 1 ranking the Hoosiers had achieved for the first time in the Knight era seven weeks earlier and built to unanimous votes before January was out.

Knight had played the last 20 minutes without making a substitution. Laskowski stepped into May's spot and the Hoosiers played to the wire. Benson had 18 points and 14 rebounds, Buckner 16 points and 10 assists. Purdue also went most of the way with its starters. All five scored in double figures.

Indiana went from the Saturday game at Purdue to a Monday night game at Illinois. Laskowski scored 28 points, Green 30 and Benson 20 as the Hoosiers cruised, 112-89. After that one, Knight said, "As a coach, I have to be prouder of the players for this game than for any other one all year. They were playing away from home, with the league championship won, and one of the best players in the country hurt – and they just played. I think I'd be remiss in not saying something about the kind of kids they are, the way they approached the game, the way they came together."

33

(Right) A championship-clinching day at Purdue ended dismally for Scott May.

(Far right) Nothing was left to be said when a brilliant season ended in 92-90 disappointment at Dayton.

May had made the trip to Champaign to be with his teammates. He had listened along with them to a taped message from Knight's longtime friend and coaching confidant, Pete Newell. The Newell tape was part of a special, one-time experiment Knight tried with the 1974-75 team. Newell and another Knight coaching friend, Clair Bee, were regular contributors of taped messages directly to the team. Others – Red Auerbach, John Havlicek – were brought in, too, but Bee and especially Newell were virtual long-range members of the Knight coaching staff.

This one came in the morning after May was hurt. Newell, up-to-the-minute with team details, told the Hoosiers:

"It's inevitable that when you lose a player like Scott May, a team is going to feel it a lot. However, one of the fortunate things about your wonderful, great team is that you all are contributors...

"In this instance, each one of you has to just take another cinch in your belt. If each one gives a little more input, there's no doubt in my mind that the direction you've been going you'll continue to go, because this is one of the beauties of a team. There is that interdependence, and that strength you get from it: that the group is greater than the individual.

"Your main concentration should be on your defense now – just that much more alert for loose balls, for interceptions, for screening out, for helping a teammate, communicating even better. Not that you don't play great defense, but you can always play better defense... And you'll probably pick it up at the other end, too.

"Just like this last game – Green comes up with the best game he's had in weeks. I think that's great... exactly what I'm talking about. He took the challenge, and this is why you've got the record you have and why you're going to do what you're going to do this year, and that's go all the way."

It didn't quite happen, the May injury in the end more than even Hoosier will could overcome. Kentucky ousted Indiana one step short of the Final Four, 92-90. Still, the 1974-75 Hoosiers went all the way into the record book and the memory books, as one of college basketball's all-time best, and most dominant, teams.

Indiana 84 UCLA 64
St. Louis Arena St. Louis, Missouri
November 29, 1975

The tone for everything was set the first night. Perfectly.

College basketball was just beginning to learn its national television potential. Eight years earlier, UCLA (with Lew Alcindor) and Houston (with Elvin Hayes) had played a special game set up in the Houston Astrodome for national TV airing. Three years earlier, the NCAA had hit upon the Final Four format it has maintained to today: semifinals on Saturday, finals on Monday, the better to cash in big on TV.

But the 1975-76 season was the first one launched by a TV game – a natural: reigning NCAA champion UCLA against the team that felt it should have won that 1975 championship, Indiana.

The Bruins kept most of their '75 champions, but there was one major change. John Wooden, after coaching

No.		Height	Class	G-S	Pts.
42	Scott May*	6-7	Sr.	32-32	23.5
33	Tom Abernethy	6-7	Sr.	32-31	10.0
54	Kent Benson*	6-11	Jr.	32-32	17.3
21	Quinn Buckner	6-3	Sr.	32-30	8.9
20	Bob Wilkerson	6-7	Sr.	32-29	7.8
22	Wayne Radford	6-3	So.	30-2	4.7
45	Jim Crews	6-5	Sr.	31-1	3.2
23	Jim Wisman	6-2	So.	26-3	2.5
34	Rich Valavicius	6-5	Fr.	28-0	2.4
25	Bob Bender	6-3	Fr.	17-0	2.1
32	Mark Haymore	6-8	So.	13-0	1.8
43	Jim Roberson	6-9	Fr.	12-0	1.6
31	Scott Eells	6-9	Fr.	12-0	0.9

* May: College Player of Year, All-America, Big Ten MVP, All-Final Four;
May, Benson: All-Big Ten; Benson: Outstanding Player, Final Four.

(Left) Hoosiers did all the cheering in a rousing national-TV 84-64 season-opening victory over UCLA.

(Right) Tom Abernethy eludes Richard Washington to score as Indiana pulls away early in the second half.

UCLA coach Gene Bartow and Bob Knight, together in the Final Four in 1973 and in the Big Ten in 1974-75, chat before a new season is launched at St. Louis Arena.

UCLA to 10 national titles in 12 years, retired. Gene Bartow, whose Memphis State team had lost to Wooden and UCLA in the 1973 championship game, resigned after just one year at Illinois to replace Wooden.

Indiana had kept most of its team that had been roaring along unbeaten and almost unchallenged, a unanimous No. 1 in the national polls, till All-America forward Scott May broke an arm in late February. Those Hoosiers lost 92-90 in the Mideast Regional final to a Kentucky team it had routed 98-74 earlier in the year, a Kentucky team that UCLA beat 92-85 in the 1975 finals, Wooden's last game.

This game had come on with a drumbeat. NBC bought the rights and gave it an 11:40 p.m. starting time – "their best time for access to their entire network, right after the 11 o'clock news," the game's matchmaker, Metro Conference commissioner Larry Albus, said.

Almost four weeks earlier in Indianapolis, Indiana had taken on the Soviet National team, including the Belovs, Sergei and Alexander, leaders of the Soviets' controversial gold-medal victory over the U.S. at Munich in 1972. The Hoosiers won, 94-78, with May showing his physical recovery was complete by hitting 13 of 15 shots and scoring 34 points.

That left 26 days to prepare for the real opener, the biggest in IU history.

Early sparring left some nicks. UCLA forward Marques Johnson, paired with May in a matchup of exceptional 6-7, 215-pound athletes, drew two fouls in the first three minutes; Indiana guard and leader Quinn Buckner, two fouls in the first four minutes.

They played on.

May, after missing his first four shots, opened a 13-8 Hoosier lead with his first basket. Once he had the range, he was fine. He finished 15-for-24 with a game-high 33 points in what he called "the biggest game I've ever played in."

It was 36-28 at halftime, but Buckner – "He's been our leader for four years," Knight said afterward – scored the first eight Indiana points of the second half to push Bartow to a timeout at 18:07, his team suddenly down 44-30.

Two minutes later the Indiana edge was 50-32, then 20 points for the first time at 56-36 after another May basket. The lead topped at 72-46 with 6½ minutes left.

Richard Washington, a 6-10 All-America forward for the '75 champions, scored 22 of his 28 points in the second half. Johnson finished with 18 points. "I think you

(Left) Bob Knight hugs Scott May after the senior forward's 'super-brilliant night.'

(Bottom) In a Bob Knight tradition maintained through 25 years, the Hoosiers pause to hear a word from the top, from university president John Ryan.

39

saw three All-America forwards out there," Bartow said. "Scott May just had a super-brilliant night."

It was May's launch toward College Player of the Year. Hoosier center Kent Benson, who also wound up a consensus All-America pick, had 17 points and a game-high 14 rebounds. "Benson played the boards very well," Knight said, "and that was one of his major assignments."

Bartow said the Hoosiers "proved they deserved their No. 1 ranking. I think they've got four guys out there who will be first-round draft choices, and they're coached superbly." He referred to IU seniors May, Buckner and Bobby Wilkerson and junior Benson. By the time Benson had gone first in the 1977 draft, NBA selectors had proved Bartow right.

The Hoosiers came down from their peak quickly. Their second game was against Florida State, the 1971 NCAA runnerup. The Hoosiers led 24-6 after 12 minutes, 47-20 at halftime, on the way to an 83-59 victory. "I'm glad this isn't like baseball," Florida State coach Hugh Durham said. "I'd hate to play these guys in a three-game homestand."

They were to have some some off-games, some narrow escapes, far more than in their unbeaten march through the 1974-75 season. Rebound baskets by Benson in the final seconds got them into overtime for victories over Kentucky and Michigan. Notre Dame pushed them to the finish at Assembly Hall before losing, 63-60, after which Knight said, "My team needs an enema." Throughout all of 1974-75, they never trailed at halftime. On five straight Saturdays in Big Ten play, this team trailed at halftime but found the second-half answer. This Indiana team got by undefeated St. John's, 76-69, before the largest crowd ever to see a college game at Madison Square Garden (19,694, another 3,500 turned away).

The 1975-76 Hoosiers met every test. Starting with the first one.

N A T I O N A L C H A M P I O N S

Indiana University

40

Their crowning achievement was achieving their crowning: the five-game sweep through tournament opposition so tough that it ultimately brought seeding to the NCAA basketball championships.

There was no seeding until the 41st of these tournaments, in 1979. The persuasive argument was the 1976 collision of No. 1-ranked Indiana and No. 2 Marquette in the Mideast Regional finals, not in the Final Four. Before that, Indiana had beaten No. 6 Alabama.

For an Indiana team that was to take a spot in history, it was the perfect route. The Hoosiers' tournament opponents – St. John's, Alabama, Marquette, UCLA and Michigan – were strong, and strong-willed. Three had lost to this Indiana team, but each had left the court convinced it could beat these unbeatables.

The Hoosiers, No. 1-ranked all year long, went into the tournament, and to Philadelphia, with more talk of the team most likely to beat Indiana than of anything inevitable about a Hoosier championship.

And they had only one really close tournament game, 74-69 over Alabama's Southeastern Conference champions.

Alabama, fresh from a 79-64 first-round rout of North Carolina, trailed Indiana by 12 early and 37-29 at halftime, still 65-57 with just under nine minutes to go.

This was a 'Bama team that spoke of new times. Coach C.M. Newton started five black players, each of them from Alabama, each of them already in elementary school the June day in 1963 when Gov. George C. Wallace stood in the Foster Auditorium doorway on campus at Tuscaloosa to deny entrance to black students James Hood and Vivian Malone, seeking to enroll. Wallace defied a presidential order from John F. Kennedy, who activated the National Guard to implement the order – two days before Medgar Evers was killed in Mississippi. Newton integrated the Alabama basketball

(Above) Bob Knight and senior co-captains Scott May and Quinn Buckner, at the end of 'a two-year quest.'

(Right) Quinn Buckner splits the Michigan defense in Indiana's pullaway to an 86-68 championship-game victory.

Tom Abernethy's knee pains get a checkout from trainer Bob Young late in the Hoosiers' Final Four victory over UCLA.

team as soon as he could after arrival, and here he was in Baton Rouge, with a genuine chance to win a national championship. Years later, Bob Knight called that Alabama team the best team any of his Hoosier clubs had faced.

With 3:58 to go, reserve Keith McCord hit a jump shot that put Alabama ahead, 69-68.

Points were coming very, very hard by then. Newton's leader was 6-10 senior center Leon Douglas, who had a 35-point, 17-rebound game against North Carolina and Mitch Kupchak, the starting center for the U.S. Olympic team at Montreal that summer. Douglas was as good a defender as he was a rebounder and scorer. He had four fouls, but his sweeping slap turned away Scott May's bid to give Indiana the lead with a layup. But with 2:02 left, May came off a screen and sank a 17-foot jump shot that edged Indiana in front, 70-69.

Three more times Alabama had the ball but couldn't score, Indiana easing out of reach on two free throws each by Tom Abernethy (14 seconds left) and Bobby Wilkerson (6 seconds left). It was a trademark game for the '76 Hoosiers. With the game riding, they had shut Alabama out for the last 3:58.

Indiana had opened its tournament path by winning 90-70 over No. 20-ranked St. John's at Notre Dame.

In December in the Holiday Festival championship game, the Redmen had lost to Indiana, 76-69, before a record Madison Square Garden crowd when both teams were unbeaten. That game was 65-65 with five minutes left and St. John's went away from it hoping openly for a March rematch.

In the second meeting, St. John's was down 48-47 until a 10-2 Indiana surge broke the Hoosiers away. St. John's coach Lou Carnesecca was convinced. He called Indiana "one of the great teams in quite a few years."

May, who already had been named College Player of the Year, had 33 points against St. John's and 25 in the Alabama game. In the headline game against Marquette (27-1 with 23 wins in a row after a December loss to Minnesota), he was on the bench with three fouls after just over six minutes of play. Indiana, up 30-19, led just 36-35 at halftime and fell behind when Lloyd Walton scored opening the second half for Marquette. Three straight May jump shots put Indiana back in command in a 65-56 victory that broke open in the last 25 seconds.

At Philadelphia, the Hoosiers' opening matchup was with reigning NCAA champion UCLA, which had gone away from its season-opening 84-64 loss to Indiana vowing to do better in a return match. Barely a minute and a half into the game at The Spectrum, UCLA picked up a second foul on Benson, a key to Hoosier operations.

Knight shifted Abernethy onto 6-11 UCLA All-American Richard Washington, got a 19-rebound performance from guard Wilkerson and watched his team roll to a solid 65-51 victory – the first time in 10 years anyone had beaten UCLA twice in a season.

Michigan – 25-4 against everyone but Indiana – ended an unbeaten season for Rutgers, 86-70. For the first time, two teams from the same conference would play for the national championship.

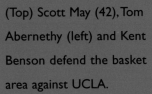

(Top) Scott May (42), Tom Abernethy (left) and Kent Benson defend the basket area against UCLA.

(Bottom) A timeout at the Final Four is no different from one in Assembly Hall for Bob Knight, Quinn Buckner and Scott May.

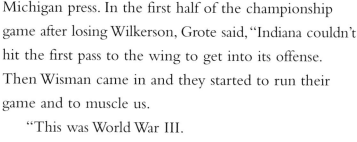

A 72-67 overtime escape from Michigan at Assembly Hall unquestionably had been the Hoosiers' closest brush with defeat in regular-season play in two years. Earlier at Ann Arbor, the Hoosiers had jumped out 16-2 and won, 80-74.

This time, Indiana lost Wilkerson to a concussion in the game's third minute. At halftime, the Hoosiers were down, 35-29, and it was 51-51 with 10 minutes left.

The game rarely has been played better than Indiana's 1976 champions played it that last 10 minutes: a 35-17 edge created by an offense that wouldn't be denied and a defense that wouldn't be dented.

May finished with 26 points and Benson 25. Benson was named the tournament's Most Outstanding Player, and he made the All-Tournament team along with May and Abernethy, the first all-anything selection for the senior who had rounded out a lineup of No. 1 NBA draft picks.

Weary Michigan guard Steve Grote saluted matchup Quinn Buckner and Wilkerson stand-in Jim Wisman. "When you do the kind of things Quinn Buckner does and hit for double figures the way he did the last month of the season, he is their best," Grote said. "I'm a guard, and I have to play him. When he goes out of the game, I'm happy."

In the second Michigan game, a nationally carried photograph showed Knight grabbing Wisman by the shirt after two straight throwaways against the

(Above) Bob Knight and College Player of the Year Scott May talk.

(Below) At the end, everything was looking up for Bob Knight.

Michigan press. In the first half of the championship game after losing Wilkerson, Grote said, "Indiana couldn't hit the first pass to the wing to get into its offense. Then Wisman came in and they started to run their game and to muscle us.

"This was World War III.

"They won the first two, too."

Knight said, "I went into this game thinking about so many people who had invested so much of themselves into our program.

"I think of an 80-year-old man (retired coaching great Clair Bee) sitting up in the mountains in New York watching this game on television. Nobody has been more influential on my basketball life than he has been.

"I think of my college coach, Fred Taylor. Not a person out there in the Indiana crowd was rooting harder for us than he was. I think of Pete Newell, Stu Inman…And today, John Havlicek came to our game and spoke to our team in its pregame meeting on what it's like to play in a championship game, and what it would be like to win.

"I went into this game thinking of all those people, and our kids. They played five damned good basketball teams in this tournament and won the championship.

"It's been kind of a two-year quest for us," Knight said.

"These kids are very, very deserving. I know better than anybody how hard and how long they have worked for this."

(Top left) Tom Abernethy's drive to All-Final Four included this drive.

(Bottom left) Kent Benson powers in a basket over 7-foot Ralph Drollinger of UCLA.

(Top right) Kent Benson's strength always was a problem for quick but undersized Michigan center Phil Hubbard.

(Bottom right) Scott May hit six straight free throws in his 26-point final-game contribution.

Indiana 73   Michigan 64

Assembly Hall

February 13, 1977

Bob Knight talks, assistant Bob Weltlich scratches his head.

All around him, all year long, there were new faces. There also was something else new in the basketball life of Kent Benson. Defeat. With painful frequency.

Benson was the one holdover starter when the other leaders of Indiana's 1975-76 Perfect Season moved on to the NBA. Benson could have gone, too. The 6-foot-9 Hoosier center, a consensus All-America pick as a junior and winner of the Outstanding Player Award at the Final Four, knew he would go high in the draft if he opted to enter it, possibly even first. But he had played out that national championship season with a wrist condition that needed surgery. Immediately after the celebrating stopped in April 1976, Benson told Hoosier coach Bob Knight that he would be back for his senior year. Then he had the surgery that took him out of the summer Olympic picture.

And when the start of practice came, Benson was fine but all his pals were gone. "He has to understand that on this team there is a tremendous burden on his shoulders," Knight said.

Part of the problem Benson and all the 1976-77 Hoosiers faced was a schedule packed with payback teams. One-by-one, the new Indiana team shed streaks left over by the one that had just left.

In the second game of the season, a road trip to Toledo to help the Mid-American Conference Rockets

No.		Height	Class	G-S	Pts.
42	Mike Woodson	6-5	Fr.	27-25	18.5
40	Glen Grunwald	6-9	Fr.	26-12	3.6
54	Kent Benson*	6-11	Sr.	23-23	19.8
22	Wayne Radford	6-3	Jr.	27-14	9.2
23	Jim Wisman	6-2	Jr.	26-21	6.3
34	Rich Valavicius	6-5	So.	18-9	4.0
41	Butch Carter	6-5	Fr.	23-13	2.9
20	Bill Cunningham	6-4	Fr.	19-8	5.1
44	Derek Holcomb	6-11	Fr.	22-4	3.9
43	Jim Roberson	6-9	So.	23-4	3.0
31	Scott Eells	6-9	So.	21-1	1.4
45	Mike Miday	6-8	Fr.	3-1	6.0
33	Trent Smock	6-5	Sr.	1-0	7.0

* Benson: MVP, Big Ten MVP, All-Big Ten, All-America.

46

(Top) Kent Benson defends against Miami guard John Shoemaker's drive.

(Bottom left) On Kent Benson's final day as a Hoosier, he controls a jump ball.

(Bottom right) Mike Woodson's 26 points helped beat No. 4 Michigan and contributed to Woodson's Big Ten-record 22.0 freshman scoring average.

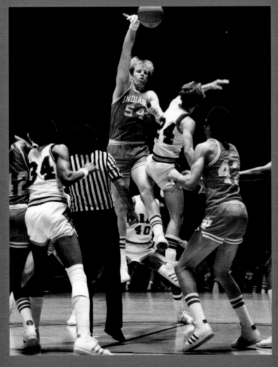

dedicate their $7-million new arena, a 59-57 loss ended the second-longest winning streak in Big Ten history: 33 games, the 32 from 1975-76 and a 110-64 opening victory over South Dakota.

In the third game, the Hoosiers lost to Kentucky 66-51, ending a 36-game streak in Assembly Hall.

In the Big Ten opener, the Hoosiers lost at home to Purdue, 80-63, the end to the most glorious of all the streaks: 37 straight conference victories, 10 beyond the former record (by the Ohio State teams on which Knight played). The Hoosiers put back-to-back 18-0 seasons together. In 24 years of 18-game Big Ten schedules, those are the only unbeaten seasons. And, in 92 years of Big Ten basketball, that is the only time a team went unbeaten two straight league seasons. The Hoosiers' average winning margin through the 37 games was 18.7, including a league-record 22.7 in 1974-75.

The one-sided home loss to Purdue showed how times had changed.

The league around Indiana hadn't declined in strength. Michigan with four starters from its 1976 NCAA runnerup, was to finish the season ranked No. 1 in the land.

Michigan had never won at Assembly Hall when it went to work on a Sunday afternoon before NBC's national cameras. The Wolverines were 11-1 and solidly out front in the Big Ten race, 18-2 overall and No. 4 in the polls. Indiana was 11-8 overall, fourth in the league at 6-4, including an 89-84 loss at Michigan 10 days before.

At halftime in this one, Michigan led 39-36. Benson and the freshman who had emerged as one of the league's top players, Mike Woodson, had three fouls each for Indiana. So did Michigan's counter to Benson, 1976 Olympian Phil Hubbard.

Hubbard's foul vulnerability was the reason Michigan coach Johnny Orr opened the second half in a 1-2-2 zone. It didn't work.

Woodson hit three straight field goals and Indiana led, 42-39. The Hoosiers led 46-41 when Benson drew his fourth foul, 15:11 left. Knight made a decision

rare for him. Benson stayed in. "I thought we were better off trying to build the lead on up and then trying to hold it if he fouled out," Knight said.

The lead reached 64-53 with just over six minutes left. With 3:48 to go and Indiana leading 65-57, Hubbard drove, Benson defended, they collided, and whistles blew. It was Hubbard's fifth foul, the backbreaker in Indiana's 73-64 win. In five Benson-Hubbard matchups, including the national championship game, the shorter, slimmer, quicker Hubbard fouled out every time.

For the drastic difference in the Indiana playing cast, the game had remarkable resemblances to the '76 national championship matchup. Michigan led 35-29 at halftime in Philadelphia, 39-36 here. Benson had 25 points at Philadelphia, 24 here. Scott May, who had 26 championship-game points, was gone, but the man wearing his No. 42, Woodson, this game had 26 points – on his way to what still is the highest Big Ten average for a freshman, 22.0.

"These kids have worked hard as hell," Knight said. "They hadn't really beaten a team on Michigan's level this year. This is a kind of dessert for them."

Benson missed the year's last four games, after a back injury at Purdue that required surgery. The Hoosiers lost three of those last five games and finished fourth, but league coaches still voted Benson the Silver Basketball that goes to the Big Ten's MVP. Milwaukee made him the No. 1 pick in the NBA draft.

16-11; Big Ten 11-7, Fourth		
South Dakota	W	110-64
at Toledo	L	57-59
Kentucky	L	51-66
at Notre Dame	L	65-78
DePaul [1]	W	50-42
Utah State [2]	W	79-71
Miami, Ohio [2]	W	76-55
Georgia [3]	W	74-52
Cincinnati [3]	L	43-52
Purdue	L	63-80
Illinois	W	80-60
at Northwestern	W	78-53
at Wisconsin	W	79-64
Michigan State	L	60-61
at Ohio State	W	79-56
Minnesota [f]	L	60-79
Iowa	W	81-65
at Michigan	L	84-89
at Michigan State	W	81-79
Michigan	W	73-64
at Minnesota [f]	L	61-65
at Illinois	L	69-73
at Purdue	L	78-86
Wisconsin	L	64-66
Northwestern	W	69-54
at Iowa	L	73-80
Ohio State	W	75-69

[f] Game forfeited to Indiana
[1] at Indianapolis
[2] Indiana Classic
[3] Sugar Bowl, New Orleans

(Far left) Wayne Radford stakes a muscular claim to a loose ball against DePaul at Market Square Arena in Radford's hometown, Indianapolis.

(Left) Governor Otis Bowen is the trophy presenter to Bob Knight and MVP-captain Kent Benson at the Indiana Classic.

Indiana 67   Notre Dame 66
Assembly Hall
December 14, 1977

Maybe the biggest of Wayne Radford's 922 Indiana University points was the only point he scored on a night when he had problems even thinking about basketball.

Radford wasn't big in Bob Knight's plans when he set up his young team to meet No. 2-ranked Notre Dame. The Irish were 6-0, fresh from a 69-66 victory over UCLA at Pauley Pavilion. Digger Phelps' roster included several players who later would be pros:

No.		Height	Class	G-S	Pts.
42	Mike Woodson	6-5	So.	29-28	19.9
34	Steve Risley	6-8	Fr.	28-11	5.2
45	Ray Tolbert	6-9	Fr.	29-28	10.1
22	Wayne Radford	6-3	Sr.	29-25	15.6
23	Jim Wisman	6-2	Sr.	29-22	4.0
40	Glen Grunwald	6-9	So.	24-11	2.5
31	Scott Eells	6-9	Jr.	22-6	4.4
41	Butch Carter	6-5	So.	29-6	2.9
25	Tommy Baker	6-1	Fr.	28-7	3.1
43	Jim Roberson	6-9	Jr.	26-1	1.7
44	Phil Isenbarger	6-8	Fr.	16-0	2.4
33	Eric Kirchner	6-7	Fr.	12-0	0.4
20	Bill Cunningham	6-4	So.	8-0	1.8

Bill Laimbeer, Kelly Tripucka, Bill Hanzlik, Tracy Jackson, Dave Batton, "Duck" Williams, Bruce Flowers. The poll standing, highest ever for a visiting team at Assembly Hall, was legitimate.

The Irish also had reason to feel lucky. Not Luck of the Irish-lucky. Not basketball-lucky. Fate-lucky.

The night before this game, a Tuesday December night when rain bordered on sleet, and wind and fog made

Bob Knight, Soviet Union coach Alexander Gomelsky chat.

Wayne Radford readies the
free throw that felled
No. 2-ranked Notre Dame.

21-8; Big Ten 12-6, Second

East Carolina	W	75-59
at Kentucky	L	64-78
Murray State	W	85-61
Notre Dame	W	67-66
SMU [1]	W	56-51
Bowling Green [2]	W	89-52
Alabama [2]	W	66-57
Jacksonville [3]	W	69-59
Florida [2]	W	73-60
Iowa	W	69-51
Illinois	L	64-65
at Minnesota	L	62-75
at Wisconsin	L	65-78
Ohio State	W	77-63
at Purdue	L	67-77
at Michigan	L	73-92
Michigan State	W	71-66
at Northwestern	W	86-70
at Michigan State	L	59-68
Purdue	W	65-64
Northwestern	W	86-62
at Ohio State	W	83-70
Michigan	W	71-59
Wisconsin	W	58-54
Minnesota	W	68-47
at Illinois	W	77-68
at Iowa	W	71-55
N C A A		
Furman [4]	W	63-62
Villanova [5]	L	60-61

[1] *at Indianapolis*
[2] *Indiana Classic*
[3] *Gator Bowl, Jacksonville, Florida*
[4] *at Charlotte, North Carolina*
[5] *at Providence, Rhode Island*

traveling even more perilous, the Irish were scheduled to fly into Bloomington in a chartered plane. Landing in Bloomington might be questionable, because of the weather, Notre Dame officials were advised. The flight was cancelled; Notre Dame bused to Bloomington. The DC-3 had been double-booked for that evening. The crew went straight to Evansville instead. The Evansville team got aboard to fly to Middle Tennessee. In the same kind of weather, on the outskirts of Evansville, seconds after takeoff, the plane crashed and all 29 aboard were killed.

"I lost a good friend," Radford said after the game.

"John Ed Washington and I lived across the street from each other from sixth grade on. Later, we moved to the north side." That was in Indianapolis, where Radford eventually played for Arlington and Washington – one of the 14 Evansville players to die in the crash – played for Tech.

"He and I stayed close," Radford said. "Every time we were home, we got in touch."

At about 10:30, about to go to bed with the big game coming up, Radford heard a TV news bulletin about the crash. About an hour later, Radford's brother called with confirmation that Washington had died.

Radford, a 6-3 senior and the team's most experienced player, had started the first two games but lost his

Crowd pleaser Ray Tolbert dunks home a basket against No. 2-ranked Notre Dame.

front-line position to sophomore Glen Grunwald, a 6-9 man moving in alongside freshmen Steve Risley (6-8) and Ray Tolbert (6-9). Despite the size, Notre Dame had six offensive-rebound baskets in getting to halftime tied 37-37.

Knight's halftime lecture focused on those cardinal sins. "In the second half, we went to the boards much better," he said. "Especially Tolbert." Tolbert, the most athletic center Knight has yet had at Indiana and a crowd favorite for his dunks, had eight rebounds the second half, 10 for the game.

Indiana led 64-62 after Tolbert's fifth foul, with 2:55 left. That's when Radford went in, for the first time. Half a minute later, the score was tied. Then it was 66-66, with 14 seconds left and Indiana in possession.

The play Knight set up during a timeout was sopho-more scoring star Mike Woodson coming off a maze of screens to take a pass from Jim Wisman for a jump shot. Wisman saw Woodson covered, went in the air for a jump shot, and with Radford's man coming at him, "just laid the ball off" to Radford.

The hard, tough Laimbeer of future Pistons notoriety surfaced. "Radford had a layup," Laimbeer said. "I just draped myself all over him."

Radford, who hadn't taken a shot in the game's first 39 minutes and 56 seconds, stood at the free-throw line with four seconds to go in a tie game. And he missed with his first try.

Bob Knight, a man of the hour after another Indiana victory at Assembly Hall.

"What was I thinking about?" Radford said. "John Ed Washington. I wanted to hit it for him."

He did, Tripucka barely missed on a 30-foot buzzer shot, and Indiana had won.

Radford didn't move into the starting lineup immediately. But, he had 24 points when the Hoosiers beat Alabama; 30 in a 71-59 victory over Michigan; 31 in a 77-68 win at Illinois. He averaged 21 points a game over the last 13 games and teamed with Woodson to lead the whole Hoosier team on a 10-1 closing charge that salvaged a second-place tie. Indiana was in the NCAA tournament for the first time since the 1976 glory.

Wayne Radford, the last Hoosier used in the Notre Dame game that his free throw won, was the 21-8 team's MVP.

53

Exuberant Ray Tolbert (45) and Glen Grunwald (40) run back on defense after a Hoosier score.

Indiana 72   Illinois 60
Assembly Hall   Champaign, Illinois
March 3, 1979

W hen Indiana cashed in on its 63-1 two-year mid-'70s march through the Big Ten and nation with a recruiting sweep of '76 midwestern seniors, the national attention went to four-year Illinois all-stater Glen Grunwald, to Ohio Player of the Year Butch Carter, and to Illinois 7-footer Derek Holcomb. Illinois coach Lou Henson was the lone outsider who said Mike Woodson might turn out to be the best of the group.

No.		Height	Class	G-S	Pts.
42	Mike Woodson	6-5	Jr.	34-33	21.0
34	Steve Risley	6-8	So.	32-15	6.6
45	Ray Tolbert	6-9	So.	34-32	12.0
24	Randy Wittman	6-5	Fr.	34-32	7.1
41	Butch Carter	6-5	Jr.	33-29	8.5
32	Landon Turner	6-9	Fr.	33-13	5.5
31	Scott Eells	6-9	Sr.	34-4	3.4
44	Phil Isenbarger	6-8	So.	21-2	2.0
22	Steve Reish	6-2	Jr.	11-0	1.7
33	Eric Kirchner	6-7	So.	13-0	0.8
25	Tommy Baker	6-1	So.	5-5	5.2
43	Jim Roberson	6-9	Sr.	6-4	3.5
23	Don Cox	6-6	So.	4-1	2.0

Ray Tolbert (45) and Landon Turner (32) gave Indiana a big inside force for three years, and Randy Wittman (right) was a major outside contributor for four years.

Woodson, who had averaged 30 points a game his senior year at Indianapolis Broad Ripple, proved Henson right from almost his first day in IU gear. But when Woodson's junior year was ending and Indiana was down to its last, slim chance to get in on post-season play, Henson saw Woodson at his greatest.

Indiana won that last-day game at Champaign's Assembly Hall, 72-60, with 48 points – still the most ever by a Bob Knight player – from Woodson.

Tumultuous understates the kind of year it had been for both Woodson and the Hoosiers. The bottom dropped out in December when Knight learned season-opening losses to Pepperdine and Texas A&M weren't the worst thing that happened to his team in the first Seawolf Classic at Anchorage. Details of marijuana use, primarily but not only there, came to Knight two weeks later. Outwardly tough, inwardly crushed, Knight dropped three players and put virtually the rest of the shaken team on probation. *His* probation. Straight-line strict.

54

(Top) Mike Woodson had his down moments but led Indiana to an NIT victory over unbeaten Alcorn State, and to the tournament championship.

55

(Bottom) A what's next gesture for Bob Knight on a chilly, losing night at Purdue.

(Above right) Landon Turner beats James Griffin, Neil Bresnahan for a rare non-Woodson basket at Illinois.

(Right) Mike Woodson twists for two on his 48-point day at Illinois.

The reduced roster delivered a shocker five days later. No. 6 Kentucky came into Assembly Hall and Indiana, with a game plan focused on getting Woodson shots, beat the Wildcats in overtime, 68-67. Woodson played all but 12 seconds of that game and scored 27 points, including the two free throws with five seconds left that put Indiana up 68-65 and clinched victory. "I've never been happier for a bunch of kids than I am after this game," Knight said. "This was a day they earned, after all the heartaches and the soul-searching of the week."

Woodson could carry the Hoosiers only so far. Three times, he led the charge against the Michigan State team that Earvin Johnson was to lead to the national championship. Woodson had 23, 24 and 25, but Michigan State won all three games. MSU coach Jud Heathcote called Woodson "a super player...the best offensive forward in the Big Ten."

The Hoosiers lost their Big Ten opener at home to Illinois; got snowed in for a day, then lost embarrassingly at Iowa, 90-61. They were 1-4 when freshman Landon Turner pushed his way into the lineup to join Ray Tolbert for a big and mobile front-court complement to the 6-5 Woodson. After the third loss to Michigan State, the Hoosiers were seventh in the Big Ten (6-7), all but

For NIT booster Bob Knight,
a long year, a happy finish.

dead for post-season with a 14-11 record at a time when only two teams from a league could go to the 40-team NCAA and the 24-team NIT had its pick from the rest.

NIT people love Knight, and the feeling – dating to his early coaching years at Army, when the NIT was the Cadets' biggest objective every year – is reciprocated. But even the NIT door was almost closed to 17-12 Indiana when it closed its season at Champaign against an Illinois team that had started this season 15-0 and flirted with No. 1 ranking, an Illini team that *was* No. 1 nationally in field-goal defense.

Woodson kicked that NIT door open.

He took four shots and put his team up 8-0. At halftime, he was 13-for-16 with 29 points, and his team led 37-32. Five minutes into the second half, he led Illinois 37-36, but the whole Hoosier team had added just 10 points more. Woodson's 48th point came on a free throw with 52 seconds left. He never took a crack at 50, passing to Carter for the game's last basket.

Woodson had a 44-point game in high school, later a 44-point game for Kansas City in the NBA. The 48 was his career peak.

"Steve Downing's 47-point game against Kentucky ranks as the all-time greatest performance I've ever

seen," Knight said, "because Steve also had 25 rebounds. But Mike was just outstanding in this game."

The Hoosiers went home, and the next day the NIT invitation came: the 18-12 overture, to the team with the worst record of all 64 with post-season chances.

The Hoosiers made the most of theirs. They went to Texas Tech, shot a school-record .711 and routed the Raiders, 78-59. Back home, unbeaten Alcorn State fell, 73-69; in the semifinals at Madison Square Garden, Ohio State was hurdled, 64-55. And, in the championship game, Tolbert and Turner combined to check Purdue All-America Joe Barry Carroll with 14 points, Carter hit a shot from the top of the key with six seconds to go, and the Hoosiers won the NIT championship, 53-52.

Carter and Tolbert were named co-MVPs for their final-game roles, but Woodson's scoring was the fuel in the Hoosier drive. At Lubbock, after Woodson had followed his 48-point game with 30 points (and 11-for-14 shooting), a Texas writer asked Knight, "You don't think he's just on a hot streak right now?"

"He has averaged 20 points a game for 90 games now," Knight said. "That's a hell of a streak."

Indiana 76 Ohio State 73 Overtime

Assembly Hall

March 2, 1980

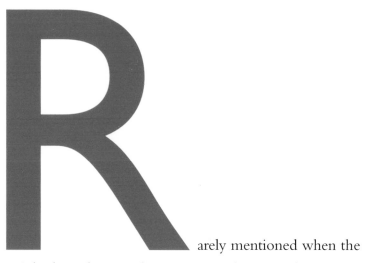

Rarely mentioned when the might-have-been Indiana NCAA championships are listed is 1980. That's definitely a Hoosier title that might have been.

The chance died early.

The Hoosiers were No. 1-ranked, 4-0 with a 23.3 average margin, when they went to Kentucky, jumped 13 points ahead in the first half but lost, 69-58. In that

From Bob Knight, a pat on the back(side).

No.		Height	Class	G-S	Pts.
42	Mike Woodson*	6-5	Sr.	14-14	19.3
45	Ray Tolbert	6-9	Jr.	29-28	10.3
32	Landon Turner	6-10	So.	26-12	7.4
11	Isiah Thomas	6-1	Fr.	29-29	14.6
41	Butch Carter	6-5	Sr.	29-23	11.1
54	Steve Bouchie	6-8	Fr.	22-16	6.5
34	Steve Risley	6-8	Jr.	27-3	2.4
44	Phil Isenbarger	6-8	Jr.	24-5	2.8
20	Jim Thomas	6-3	Fr.	21-2	2.7
40	Glen Grunwald	6-9	Jr.	26-4	1.7
30	Ted Kitchel	6-8	Fr.	22-4	1.8
31	Tony Brown	6-2	Fr.	17-0	1.0
23	Chuck Franz	6-2	Fr.	20-0	0.7
24	Randy Wittman	6-6	So.	5-5	5.8

* Big Ten MVP

game, third-year guard Randy Wittman went out early with a foot injury that was confirmed later as a stress fracture. His season ended that night.

Mike Woodson, a likely All-American after following his standout junior season with brilliant play for the U.S. team that won the Pan American Games gold medal in San Juan, Puerto Rico, for the U.S. and coach Bob Knight, also came out of the Kentucky game ailing. He played one more game, scoring 19 points against Toledo, before back problems forced him to surgery. The Hoosiers had lost two of college basketball's best players.

They weren't destitute. Recruiting had added one of the best players in the history of the game. Freshman guard Isiah Thomas had excelled with Woodson in the

(Far left) With the Big Ten championship at stake, Ray Tolbert (45) battles Ohio State's Herb Williams and Jim Smith (23) for a rebound.

(Left) Freshman Isiah Thomas challenges Herb Williams on a 21-point, 10-rebound, 7-assist, big-victory day for Thomas.

(Left) Mike Woodson's 24-point contribution to a 65-61 victory over Michigan and Mike McGee (40) was part of the 6-0 Indiana stretch run that earned the Hoosiers the Big Ten championship and Woodson the league's MVP award.

(Right) Bob Knight and assistant Jim Crews study a Hoosier practice.

tense gold-medal game at San Juan. He had things to learn, experience to gain, but even as a rookie he was a third reason why the 1980 NCAA title was in Hoosier grasp.

There were enough more of those reasons – big men Ray Tolbert and Landon Turner, guards Butch Carter and Jim Thomas, shooter Ted Kitchel, rookies Steve Bouchie and Tony Brown, experienced frontcourt reserves Steve Risley and Glen Grunwald – that the Hoosiers stayed alive in the strong Big Ten even without Woodson and Wittman.

But the breathing was labored.

The opening weekend of the league season, the Hoosiers lost 59-58 at Ohio State and 52-50 at Wisconsin – each time to last-minute points. When six weeks into the conference season Illinois routed the Hoosiers, 89-68, at Champaign, Indiana was 7-5, but just one game back of co-leaders Ohio State and Purdue.

And then, on Valentine's Day at Iowa City, Woodson returned – seven weeks to the day after he had undergone surgery to remove a ruptured disc.

Barely a minute into the game, Woodson slipped behind a screen, took a pass from Kitchel and sank his first jump shot of the league season. He also hit his second shot. And his third. Years later when Isiah Thomas was named MVP of the NBA All-Star game, Thomas was asked if that was his biggest basketball thrill. No, he said. "My biggest was watching Mike Woodson come back from back surgery and hit his first three shots at Iowa."

Woodson went on to score 20 points that night, and

Indiana won 66-55. He wasn't the old Woodson, of tip-top shape, but he scored 24 points and Minnesota fell; 20, and the Hoosiers won 75-72 at Michigan State; 24, and Indiana won 65-61 at Michigan; 16, and the Hoosiers got by Wisconsin, 61-52. Along the way, Purdue had lost three times and Ohio State once.

So when the Buckeyes and Hoosiers met at Assembly Hall on national TV on the final Sunday afternoon of the season, it was a Big Ten championship game. Each came in 12-5; no other team was in the picture.

It turned out to be a lovely picture. When the time comes to pick the best game ever played at Assembly Hall, Indiana's 76-73 overtime victory over Ohio State for the 1980 Big Ten championship may come out No. 1.

There was some talent out there. Only 13 players got into the game. Six became first-round NBA draft picks (Herb Williams, Kelvin Ransey and Clark Kellogg of Ohio State; Woodson, Tolbert and Isiah Thomas of Indiana). Three more played at least a year in the NBA (Ohio State's Jim Smith and Granville Waiters, Indiana's Butch Carter). A 10th, Indiana's Turner, was a sure first-rounder till his playing career ended in a 1981 auto crash that left him paralyzed.

Woodson was the only one who on the last day of the season still was trying to play his way into shape. "My quickness is not as good as it was," he said this day. "I get tired kind of easily. I don't feel any pain, but my legs aren't as good as they were before the surgery, and that affects my shot."

21-8; Big Ten 13-5, Champion

Miami, Ohio	W	80-52
Xavier [1]	W	92-66
Texas-El Paso [1]	W	75-43
Georgetown	W	76-69
at Kentucky	L	58-69
Toledo [2]	W	80-56
North Carolina	L	57-61
Tennessee [3]	W	70-68
Brown [3]	W	61-52
at Ohio State	L	58-59
at Wisconsin	L	50-52
Michigan	*W	63-61
Michigan State	W	72-64
Iowa	W	81-69
at Northwestern	W	81-72
at Minnesota	L	47-55
Purdue	W	69-58
Illinois	W	60-54
at Purdue	L	51-56
Northwestern	W	83-69
at Illinois	L	68-89
at Iowa	W	66-55
Minnesota	W	67-54
at Michigan State	W	75-72
at Michigan	W	65-61
Wisconsin	W	61-52
Ohio State	*W	76-73

N	C	A	A
Virginia Tech [4]		W	68-59
Purdue [5]		L	69-76

* Overtime
[1] Indiana Classic
[2] at Indianapolis
[3] Cabrillo Classic, San Diego
[4] at Bowling Green, Kentucky
[5] at Lexington, Kentucky

So all he did in this intense and tense game was play all 45 minutes and score 21 points.

There were some brilliant plays in the bristling game.

Ohio State jumped out 10-3, but it was 10-9 when the 6-5 Woodson reached from behind to strip away a jump shot by the 6-11 Williams. Woodson landed, planted and threw a 50-foot pass to Carter for a 3-point play and Indiana's first lead.

Thomas, maybe college basketball's all-time best at converting a one-on-two break, centered a four-on-one break early in the second half. The one back was Williams, who maneuvered with the slippery Thomas, went up with him to block his shot, retrieved the ball and launched a pass to Smith for a dunk.

Thomas, just 6-1, dived in among the giants for one of his 10 rebounds, wheeled out of the pack to lead a fast break, and laid a pass off to Tolbert for a dunk. Retired Marquette coach Al McGuire was working the game for TV. On the first white paper he could find, ironically an Ohio State press guide, McGuire scratched: "Isiah Thomas – Franchise."

Ohio State had started a surge with the Williams play and opened a 59-51 lead seconds before the Thomas play. Just ahead of it, and just after it, Woodson

hit jump shots, and the Hoosiers were close again.

With 47 seconds left, Kellogg drove the middle and backhanded a shot home for a 65-63 lead. Indiana worked patiently for a tying shot. "We almost took too much time," Knight said later. Tolbert finally got a shot from close range, but he missed. Carter, the one Ohioan playing for Indiana, grabbed the rebound and was on his way back up to tie the game when Williams fouled him – No. 5 for the Buckeye center.

With seven seconds to go, Carter had his chance to tie the game. "I didn't want to be long," he said. "If anything, short, because I always get a good bounce. I would have had a chance for it to bounce in." He swished both, and the game went into overtime, minus Williams.

Indiana jumped out 69-65 just 40 seconds into overtime, but the Hoosier lead was 72-71 when Carter went back to the line under extreme pressure: 13 seconds left, one-and-one. Of course, Ohio State coach Eldon Miller took an "icing" timeout. Of course, Knight drew up defensive plans, for after "you make these two free throws." Woodson, stationed at deep safety, was as confident in Carter as Knight was. "Butch is a senior," Woodson said. "He's been through quite a bit. He knows what it takes to win."

Isiah, all charged up.

For Bob Knight, lunchtime in the '70s and '80s meant Smitty's Southside Cafe.

At that particular moment, it took two free throws. Carter delivered them, and before Ohio State could score again, rookie Thomas made the lead a padlocked 76-71 at 0:04, as four-year teammates Woodson and Carter clasped hands and grinned in backcourt.

Thomas that day came close to something that has never happened yet for a Hoosier: a triple-double. He had 21 points, 10 rebounds and 7 assists.

All over the court, numbers glistened. Williams had 18 points and 11 rebounds, Kellogg 18 points and 16 rebounds, Ransey 17 points and 7 assists, Tolbert 10 points and 12 rebounds, Carter 12 points and those four immense free throws. In 45 relentless minutes, the two teams combined for just 19 turnovers, 11 of them by Indiana.

And the Hoosiers were Big Ten champions.

They were champions because they went 6-0 after Woodson's return. No other team in the entire Big Ten season put six straight wins together. "How," Knight said after the game, "could anyone else be the Big Ten's MVP?"

No one else was. In a conferencewide vote surely unprecedented, the man who played just a third of the Big Ten season was named the league's Most Valuable Player.

Down that stretch, every game competitive and close, he averaged 20.3 points a game and 40.2 minutes a game.

The Hoosiers and their exhausted star for one of the rare times reached the NCAA tournament on the other side of a peak. They survived Virginia Tech, 68-59, but sank 19 points behind Purdue and fell, 76-69. Purdue went on to the Final Four, and Louisville won the championship.

With a different roll of the dice, with full, healthy contributions from Woodson and Wittman, who knows?

Certainly, fate had the pieces in place for a perfect Woodson finish. The Final Four that year was in his hometown, Indianapolis. And the championship game was played on his 22nd birthday.

63

The trophies already have started to accumulate outside Bob Knight's uncluttered office.

Indiana 69   Illinois 66
Assembly Hall   Champaign, Illinois
March 5, 1981

T he last week of the season began with their NCAA tournament spot uncertain. Indiana's Hoosiers were 19-9 with two road games left, tough ones, at Illinois and Michigan State. The national coaches' poll had them 13th, which seemed generous. No other team in the Top 20 had lost nine times.

It had been a long and trying, mostly unsatisfying

Bob Knight and Isiah Thomas, finding the answers to a national championship.

No.		Height	Class	G-S	Pts.
45	Ray Tolbert*	6-9	Sr.	35-35	12.2
30	Ted Kitchel	6-8	So.	34-27	9.2
32	Landon Turner*	6-10	Jr.	33-18	9.5
11	Isiah Thomas*	6-1	So.	34-34	16.0
24	Randy Wittman	6-6	So.	35-32	10.4
20	Jim Thomas*	6-3	So.	33-10	3.7
31	Tony Brown	6-2	So.	28-8	3.3
34	Steve Risley	6-8	Sr.	31-8	3.0
40	Glen Grunwald	6-9	Sr.	27-1	1.9
54	Steve Bouchie	6-8	So.	29-2	1.6
44	Phil Isenbarger	6-8	Sr.	26-0	1.7
23	Chuck Franz	6-2	So.	21-0	1.3
43	Mike LaFave	6-9	Fr.	15-0	0.7
42	Craig Bardo	6-5	Fr.	4-0	1.0

Isiah Thomas: All-America, All-Big Ten, Outstanding Player Final Four; Tolbert: Big Ten MVP; Turner, Jim Thomas: All-Final Four.

Hoosier season. Waiting on them in Champaign-Urbana was the antithesis of sympathy. Indiana and Bob Knight represented basketball subjection in Illinois, both on the court and in recruiting. Knight's best Indiana teams, the best in Big Ten history, had Chicagoan Quinn Buckner running them. Now, the Hoosiers were coming to town with another prized Chicago recruit, Isiah Thomas, as their on-court leader.

But the Illini, down so long, were rolling at 19-6 and in range to catch Indiana for second place in the league. *Champaign News-Gazette* sports editor Loren Tate called it the biggest March game at Illinois since the early '60s. Local radio stations spent game day playing an upbeat tune that captured the revolutionary spirit:

(Top left) A night to celebrate on Kirkwood in downtown Bloomington.

(Top right) Road trips make napping catch-as-catch-can for Isiah Thomas.

(Bottom left) Isiah Thomas, Ray Tolbert (45) hope Landon Turner will have a ball.

(Bottom right) Isiah Thomas works hard for an "easy" score.

(Right) A Bob Knight look, one of an infinite variety.

(Bottom right) The national-champion Hoosiers filled Assembly Hall one last time for their triumphal return.

"The '80s Belong to Illini." When that wasn't playing, callers were on the air prophesying an agonizing evening for Knight and Indiana.

Through halftime, the mood prevailed. Illinois led 32-28, and Thomas already had three fouls.

The last half, a national champion took form.

Illinois was playing well, too, and led 49-45 nearly 10 minutes into the second half. Steve Risley and Jim Thomas popped open along the baseline for shots that tied the game and moved Illini coach Lou Henson to abandon his zone defense and go after Indiana man-to-man. The Illini could play it. The basketball was beautiful. A one-point lead swung back and forth as the teams combined to score on seven straight possessions. Illinois led 56-55 and Indiana had the basketball when Knight called time out with 6:13 left.

"As long as they were in a man-to-man, we wanted to go with our spread offense," Knight said. The five Hoosiers spread out to points all over their end of the court. Twice in a row, Indiana passed the basketball till someone – first Ray Tolbert, then Risley – set a screen and Randy Wittman cut off it to take a pass and score a layup.

From 59-56, Illinois never caught up. The spread continued; the layups stopped. But the Hoosiers hit 10 straight free throws to keep Illinois forever out of catch-up range.

That satiny last half, with a packed and lusty crowd howling for victory, Indiana shot .800 from the field (12-for-15) and .944 on free throws (17-for-18). For the full game, the Hoosiers had nine turnovers; Illinois, responding with a great performance of its own, just eight.

"You just can't see a lot better game than that," Knight said. "I thought it was really well played, just an awfully good college basketball game."

And then word came in from East Lansing that Michigan State had beaten Iowa in overtime, 71-70. Great news and bad news. The Iowa loss, and Indiana's win, tied the two for the Big Ten lead with a game to go. But Indiana's remaining game was at Michigan State.

The Hoosiers were a luxury car that had coughed and wheezed its way to the finish line. They lost a spotlighted matchup with No. 1 Kentucky 68-66 after Thomas laid an alley-oop pass for Tolbert in front of the basket, but the dunk try missed. They lost at Notre Dame, at North Carolina. They went to Honolulu and lost to Clemson, 58-57, then in the consolation round to Pan American, so their record entering league play was 7-5, worst of the Knight era.

Then they lost in overtime at Michigan, by 68-66 at Purdue, and both at home (56-53) and on the road (78-65) to Iowa, the reason the Hawkeyes – who never before had won at Assembly Hall – were leading the league going into the final week.

National championship coaches Al McGuire (left) and Bob Knight share a laugh.

The loss at Iowa was a watershed game. Upset with how the Hoosiers were defending 6-5 Hawkeye forward Kevin Boyle, Knight assigned 6-foot-10 Landon Turner to him. Turner's defensive experience up to then had been almost entirely against centers, post players. About the only thing Knight saw that he liked during the crucial defeat was how well Turner stayed with Boyle. The rest of the way, Turner — so long in development — was primary in Hoosier offensive and defensive play, frequently against quick forwards.

Ironically, Illinois was his one mediocre performance in the last 10 games. Just before going to Champaign, he learned of the death of a particularly close grandfather. He didn't have a rebound that night and wasn't part of the late-game spread that won the game.

But he became the final piece in a lineup that could send two erstwhile centers, Turner and 6-9 Ray Tolbert, out on the floor to defend forwards while 6-8 Ted Kitchel worked against post players. Thomas and Wittman gave the team guards who were (1) to win All-America honors, Thomas in this season and Wittman as a senior in 1982-83, and (2) to have long and distinguished NBA careers.

The Hoosiers went from Champaign to a crushing 69-48 final-night victory at Michigan State, after they had watched Iowa open their way to a clear-cut championship by losing at Ohio State in an afternoon game. They went into the tournament as Big Ten champions, never losing after that night at Iowa City when the full scope of Turner's potential emerged.

The closest brush was at Illinois in maybe the best-played game of the whole college basketball season.

1 9 8 0 – 1 9 8 1		
National Champion		
26-9; Big Ten 14-4, Champion		
Ball State	W	75-69
Murray State	W	59-41
Kentucky	L	66-68
at Notre Dame	L	64-68
California [1]	W	94-58
Baylor [1]	W	83-47
Oral Roberts [2]	W	65-56
at North Carolina	L	56-65
at Kansas State	W	51-44
Rutgers [3]	W	55-50
Clemson [3]	L	57-58
Pan American [3]	L	60-66
Michigan State	W	55-43
Illinois	W	78-61
at Michigan	*L	52-55
at Ohio State	W	67-60
Iowa	L	53-56
at Northwestern	W	93-56
at Minnesota	*W	56-53
Purdue	W	69-61
Wisconsin	W	89-64
at Purdue	L	66-68
Northwestern	W	86-52
at Wisconsin	W	59-52
at Iowa	L	65-78
Minnesota	W	74-63
Ohio State	W	74-58
Michigan	W	98-83
at Illinois	W	69-66
at Michigan State	W	69-48
N C A A		
Maryland [4]	W	99-64
Ala. Birmingham [5]	W	87-72
St. Joseph's, Pa [5]	W	78-46
LSU [6]	W	67-49
North Carolina [6]	W	63-50

* Overtime
[1] Indiana Classic
[2] at Indianapolis
[3] Rainbow Classic, Honolulu
[4] at Dayton, Ohio
[5] at Assembly Hall
[6] at The Spectrum, Philadelphia

Life is happy for a Hoosier in '81.

NATIONAL CHAMPIONS

Indiana University

They got together on New Year's Eve, but not for any revelry. Strictly by chance, the flights that were bringing their teams home from holiday tournaments made mid-continent switches in Kansas City with coinciding layovers. So Bob Knight of Indiana and Dean Smith of North Carolina ran into each other and drifted off into a corner, to commiserate.

Smith's team had just been drubbed, 76-60, by Minnesota in a tournament at Los Angeles. Knight's had just lost twice in the Rainbow Classic at Honolulu, the second game 66-60 to Pan American.

Theirs wasn't the body language of two coaches who would be playing for the national championship three months later.

"Bobby was telling me, 'I just can't play (Ray) Tolbert and (Landon) Turner together,'" Smith recalled.

"And I was asking him: 'Does Minnesota *always* shoot that well? From that far out?'"

Just 11 days earlier, their teams had played in Chapel Hill, and North Carolina won 65-56. Indiana also had lost to Kentucky and Notre Dame. The Hoosiers after

Isiah Thomas clips the net that he had singed for 19 second-half points in the 63-50 championship-game victory over North Carolina.

Hawaii were 7-5, the worst pre-Big Ten record for any of Knight's first 25 Indiana teams. "I *think* Indiana has a great team," Smith said after the Chapel Hill game. "Time will tell."

And time did. Just in time.

The NCAA tournament had grown to 48, three-fourths of its eventual size. Indiana went into the last two-game weekend not certain of even a spot in the field, a game back of Iowa with two to play – road

The final moments before going onto the court are no different at the Final Four from the norm throughout the Bob Knight years: a few final moments after taping for last-minute thoughts and notebook glances inside the Hoosier lockerroom, privacy somewhere nearby for Knight, this time at Philadelphia with Bill Frieder, an assistant coach under Johnny Orr on the Michigan team that played Indiana for the 1976 championship and the first-year head coach of the Wolverines himself in '81.

(Above) NBC's Dick Enberg, an Indiana University alumnus, gets some pre-Final Four information from Bob Knight and his longtime adviser, Pete Newell.

(Bottom right) Isiah Thomas won the Outstanding Player Award at the Final Four for all kinds of roles, including his usual one running the Indiana offense.

70

games at Illinois and Michigan State for Indiana, which could have slid to third with losses. Instead, the Hoosiers won twice, Iowa lost twice and Indiana was the clear-cut league champion.

The Hoosiers' 21-9 record was the worst of any of the 16 seeded teams. Indiana drew a No. 3 seed, in the Mideast Regional. The assignment was more significant than normal. Indiana was the regional host.

The Hoosiers, though, had a dangerous step to take to get to the regional. Their tournament debut was against Maryland, a talented team that cruised by Tennessee-Chattanooga, 81-69, to get out of the 16-team first round. The Terps and Hoosiers were to play at Dayton, Indiana's first return to the place where the 1975 team's dream ended, 92-90, against Kentucky. That afternoon, Knight had closed his press conference remarks: "We'll be back some day." The day had come.

The Mideast Regional looked like the toughest of all: No. 1 DePaul, No. 8 Kentucky and No. 14 Wake Forest, in addition to No. 9 Indiana. Boston College and Alabama Birmingham took out Wake Forest and Kentucky. When Indiana stepped on-court at Dayton, the arena still was abuzz over the shocker that had just ended: unseeded St. Joseph's of Pennsylvania over top-ranked DePaul, 49-48.

Two minutes into the Maryland game, Indiana was down 8-0.

A national champion emerged right there.

By halftime, Indiana led 50-34. That was after 16

turnover-free minutes with 71 percent shooting. One brief Maryland flurry cut the lead to 54-42, but a 15-point Indiana run killed any comeback dreams.

The game ended 99-64. "We just got our fannies beat," Maryland coach Lefty Driesell said. "They were the best team we've played since I got my program going. If they'd been playing the 76ers, they'd have beaten the 76ers."

Tolbert and Turner, the two big men Knight had such problems making into a tandem, combined for 46 points, 26 by Tolbert. Together they were 19-for-26 with 15 rebounds, 5 blocks and 3 steals. Isiah Thomas was 9-for-11 with 19 points and 14 assists, and no turnovers.

Back home, the Hoosiers met a tournament Cinderella. Gene Bartow had left UCLA to begin a program at Alabama Birmingham. When the green-and-gold Blazers hurdled Kentucky, 69-62, they became a tournament darling.

Assembly Hall and all, UAB was to give the Hoosiers their toughest test. Indiana trailed 25-19 more than 10 minutes into the game. With under three minutes to go, Indiana's lead was just 77-70. Isiah Thomas hit six free throws in 59 seconds, 13-for-15 in a 27-point night, and Indiana won, 87-72.

"I feel as though we could have beaten an awful lot of teams tonight," Bartow said. "To me, this was a typical Bob Knight team. They do so many things so well. I didn't see them early this year, but I've heard they were struggling a little then. They're not struggling now."

Isiah Thomas cashes in a steal opening the second half of the championship game, while Jimmy Black chases and Virginia All-American Ralph Sampson (behind Indiana coaches Jim Crews and Bob Knight) leans in to watch.

71

(Above) Bob Knight packed them in at a press conference between the semifinals and the final game.

(Bottom right) Landon Turner's legs frame a loose-ball battle in the 'coaching clinic' national

72 championship game: Indiana vs. North Carolina, Bob Knight vs. Dean Smith.

St. Joseph's had beaten Tom Davis's Boston College team, 42-41, to reach the regional finals. Hawks coach Jim Lynam loved to spread the floor and play patiently against strong teams. That was his plan in this game: "I was hoping we would be able to spread the defense and create some openings," he said. "But when we spread the floor, they had definite things in mind *they* wanted to do defensively."

Also, offensively. The Hoosiers shot an NCAA tournament-record .686 (35-for-51, including 13-for-16 by Tolbert and Turner) and won easily, 78-46.

At Philadelphia, Louisiana State was waiting. Dale Brown's Bayou Bengals had won the Southeastern Conference championship. They were 31-3 going against Indiana, No. 4 in both national polls.

With 3:14 left in the half, Indiana trailed 30-27 and Isiah Thomas drew his third foul. He left the game and Indiana didn't score again through halftime. Neither did LSU. The 30-27 score stood.

Indiana opened the second half with a 21-4 blitz and won, 67-49 – the score 40-19 over the last 20 minutes.

Isiah Thomas had gone out again after drawing his fourth foul early in the second half. His replacement was Jim Thomas, a Floridian who was the first Knight recruit from outside the Ohio-Indiana-Illinois base that had supplied him his first eight recruiting seasons.

"I had never heard of James Thomas," LSU guard Ethan Martin admitted afterward. Thomas scored just two points, but at 6-3 he had nine rebounds, two assists, two blocks and a steal. "Good night," Kansas State coach Jack Hartman said. "That kid is quicker than a cat. I was *really* impressed."

When Al Wood scored 39 points and North Carolina upset Ralph Sampson and Virginia, 78-65, coaches in the Philadelphia audience looked forward to a clinic: Knight, 40, against Smith, 50. "Two coaches who have been very successful," Hartman called them, "two who have been copied tremendously.

"There are some great matchups: Tolbert against (Sam) Perkins, Turner against (James) Worthy.

"There isn't a good matchup at the other (front-court) spot. Wood has the mobility."

That would have been against starter Ted Kitchel, who in just four minutes picked up three fouls. From the bench one more time came Jim Thomas, primarily to take on Wood.

North Carolina jumped out 16-8. "It didn't look good then," Knight said. "We were on the verge of being blown out."

Randy Wittman sank four shots over North Carolina's zone defense to give Indiana a 26-25 halftime lead. The last came from the baseline just ahead of the buzzer, Wittman uncharacteristically clapping to command the attention of Isiah Thomas for a pass.

Opening the second half, Isiah stole the ball from Jimmy Black for a layup. Seconds later, he picked off a pass and drove to an acrobatic basket. Those plays, Smith said, "broke it open. His two steals were the turning point."

Then Thomas went to work in an unusual area for a 6-1 player: posted up, around the basket. He was unstoppable, his feeder time and again his namesake and non-relative, Jim Thomas, as Indiana won, 63-50.

Isiah finished with 23 points, 19 in the last half. Jim Thomas had eight assists. He was the first non-starter ever to make the All-Final Four team, and he did it scoring just two points in each game. Isiah won the tournament's Outstanding Player Award, with 105 media votes. Jim Thomas got 15½ votes for that award.

Also on the All-Final Four team was Turner, whose late-season emergence was the Hoosiers' final key. Turner was the only Hoosier to score in double figures all five tournament games, averaging 13.2 points and 5.4 rebounds while shooting .549 from the field and .769 on free throws. It was to be his last college basketball. Four months later, an auto accident left him paralyzed from the chest down. At the end of what would have been his senior season, 1981-82, the U.S. Basketball Writers Assn. named him to an honorary position on its All-America team. That year, also, Boston Celtics general manager Red Auerbach used his last drafting spot for Turner. And, in 1984, in a wheelchair, Landon Turner went through commencement exercises at Assembly Hall and received his IU degree.

The championship game made its own controversy. About seven hours earlier, President Ronald Reagan was shot as he left a Washington luncheon. His condition at one point was more grave than reports to the public indicated. After consideration by the NCAA Tournament Committee, in consultations that included presidents of both competing schools, the decision was made to go ahead with the game, rather than postpone it. During the discussions, one proposal was to call off the game entirely and declare the two co-champions. Big Ten Commissioner Wayne Duke was the committee chairman. That, Duke said, "received no consideration."

For Ray Tolbert (45), Landon Turner (32) and a Hoosier-loving mob, there's no question who's No. 1 after the 63-50 final-game victory over North Carolina.

Indiana 58   Minnesota 55
Williams Arena   Minneapolis, Minnesota
February 6, 1982

Fate wasn't kind to the 1981-82 Indiana basketball team, which in other years with better luck would have been contending for a second straight national championship.

Instead, the leader of the '81 champions, Isiah Thomas, unsurprisingly passed up his last two years of eligibility to enter the NBA, where he was a first-year All-Star. The real jolt to Indiana basketball came in mid-summer '81 when the talent that had blossomed so well in the

No.		Height	Class	G-S	Pts.
30	Ted Kitchel*	6-8	Jr.	29-28	19.6
20	Jim Thomas	6-3	Jr.	29-25	9.2
54	Steve Bouchie	6-8	Jr.	29-17	6.4
24	Randy Wittman	6-6	Jr.	29-26	11.9
31	Tony Brown	6-2	Jr.	29-12	4.7
33	Uwe Blab	7-2	Fr.	24-10	7.5
11	Dan Dakich	6-5	Fr.	29-10	3.0
42	John Flowers	6-9	Fr.	29-8	4.7
21	Winston Morgan	6-5	Fr.	24-8	2.4
25	Cam Cameron	6-2	Jr.	15-0	1.7
23	Chuck Franz	6-2	Jr.	21-1	0.7
44	Rick Rowray	6-6	Fr.	1-0	2.0

* All-Big Ten.

hothouse of the Final Four was cut down before it could reach full bloom. Landon Turner, All-Final Four when three-time national Player of the Year Ralph Sampson wasn't, came out of a July auto crash barely alive and paralyzed from the chest down.

Already minus a senior group headed by Big Ten MVP Ray Tolbert, the Hoosiers figured to take a major fall. It bottomed out the first weekend in February when they started a road trip to Iowa (No. 5 in the land) and Minnesota (No. 6) with a 62-40 Thursday night hammering by the league-leading Hawkeyes.

No chance to go home and regroup. Late-night flight from Iowa to Minneapolis, Saturday afternoon rematch with a team already responsible for some

(Above) With Fred Taylor, his former coach now in a role as Big Ten TV analyst, Bob Knight chats – before the cameras come on.

(Right) Landon Turner's first return to Assembly Hall after his summertime auto accident brought a loud and long tribute.

(Right) Tony Brown goes high and wide against Minnesota's Mychal Thompson.

(Bottom right) Randy Wittman finds a way.

red-headed West German who had spent a high school year in Effingham, Ill., learned a little bit about U.S. basketball, and returned to spend his senior season there. Knight felt the situation was perfect for recruiting him: a year for him to work behind Turner, probably red-shirting, then after Turner's graduation advancement as quickly as he could absorb the complex new game. Turner's accident scrapped the breaking-in period. Blab was thrown into competition immediately.

Blab went to Minneapolis with a scoring average of 6.0, not too far above the grade average that ultimately made him Phi Beta Kappa. He knew better than any Hoosier fan that even the low point average didn't tell the full extent of his frustrations. "Every game when I had played a lot, we lost," he said. "Every game. I was a little upset about that. Nobody else had that."

Breuer came in averaging 17.1, with 25 straight double-figure games. Early, it became clear that the scoreless second half against Blab in Bloomington hadn't been happenstance. A 7-2 opponent's hand in his face

Hoosier horrors. Fresh ones. A week before, Minnesota had gone into Assembly Hall and thoroughly handled the Hoosiers, 69-62. Indiana was 5-2 and a game out of first place nearing the halfway mark. That loss and the humiliation at Iowa had dropped the Hoosiers to 5-4 and three games out in a race that had narrowed to just the two border rivals, Iowa and Minnesota.

And the luckless Hoosiers were dealt a visit to sold-out, noisy Williams Arena. Indiana coach Bob Knight hadn't seen many things he liked in the losses to Iowa and Minnesota, but one thing he noticed was that 7-foot-3 Minnesota center Randy Breuer, on his way to Big Ten MVP honors, had scored 15 points as Minnesota opened a 35-24 halftime lead in Bloomington, then hadn't scored the second half after Knight matched him up with his own 7-2 freshman, Uwe Blab.

Blab got his fourth start of the year at Minneapolis.

Blab – pronounced blop – was an intelligent,

Freshman Uwe Blab had to learn on the job, but by the key victory at Minnesota, "he really hurt us," Gopher coach Jim Dutcher said.

19-10; Big Ten 12-6, Second

Miami, Ohio	W	71-64
Notre Dame	W	69-55
at Kentucky	L	69-85
Colorado State [1]	W	82-41
Penn State [1]	W	80-51
Tulane [2]	W	77-59
Kansas State	W	58-49
Villanova [3]	L	59-63
Kansas [3]	L	61-71
at Michigan State	L	58-65
at Northwestern	L	61-75
Michigan	W	81-51
Ohio State	W	66-61
at Illinois	W	54-53
Purdue	W	77-55
at Wisconsin	W	62-56
Minnesota	L	62-69
at Iowa	L	40-62
at Minnesota	W	58-55
Illinois	W	73-60
Iowa	W	73-58
Wisconsin	W	88-57
at Purdue	L	65-76
at Ohio State	L	65-68
at Michigan	W	78-70
Northwestern	W	79-49
Michigan State	W	74-58
N C A A		
Robert Morris [4]	W	94-62
Ala. Birmingham [4]	L	70-80

[1] *Indiana Classic*
[2] *at Indianapolis*
[3] *Holiday Festival at New York*
[4] *at Nashville, Tennessee*

did bother him. "That's the reason I tried to keep my hand in his face, even at the cost of a foul," Blab said. Ultimately, he fouled out. "Maybe I should have backed off a little," he said, "but I didn't."

No reason to. Breuer's double-figure streak ended with a 9-point game, to rookie Blab's 18. Breuer managed just 5 rebounds; Blab, 8.

Still, Minnesota led 37-29 at halftime.

Knight had made one other lineup change for the game: freshman Winston Morgan in at guard for third-year starter Randy Wittman. Wittman, one of the best shooters in Hoosier history, was in a slump. He was 0-for-5 in the loss at Iowa; he came off the bench at Minneapolis and missed five more in a row, 14 in all including his last four shots in the home loss to Minnesota. Deadly Randy Wittman was a .385 Big Ten shooter when this game went into its stretch minutes, tight.

Three times in a row, Indiana's offense got Wittman open from long range. He hit all three. Why go to a slumping shooter then? "If Mickey Mantle had struck out seven times," Knight countered, "would you put Ralph Houk in to pinch-hit for him?"

Indiana trailed 45-41 with 12:07 left when Wittman sniped from 18 feet. The shot swished. His streak finally over, "I did feel better," Wittman said. His teammates came right back to him, from the same place. It was 45-45.

At 51-51, Blab already out on fouls, Wittman got another opening. Swish. "Wittman is a great shooter," Minnesota shooter Trent Tucker said. "For him to miss

14 in a row – I can't believe it." The three he hit and the circumstances at the time were "nice to see," Knight said. "When we needed some buckets, we went to Wittman and he got them."

Minnesota coach Jim Dutcher called Blab the difference between the two week-apart games. "He really hurt us defensively," Dutcher said. "He had Randy out of his game."

Blab "has worked like hell, and he still has a long way to go," Knight said. "We're talking about a kid from a totally different background who really had no idea what college basketball was like."

Minnesota went from there to a triple-overtime victory at Iowa and won the Big Ten title outright. Indiana went from Minneapolis to a weekend at home and a sweep over Illinois and Iowa, with Ted Kitchel scoring 34 and 33 points. The Hoosiers were 7-2 on the "back nine" of their Big Ten schedule to pull out a second-place tie with Iowa and get an NCAA berth. When they won their tournament opener from Robert Morris, they became the first reigning NCAA champion in six years to win even one tournament game the following year. But their reign and their 19-10 season ended in Round 2, 80-70 to the Alabama Birmingham team that had given the 1981 champions their toughest tournament challenge.

Indiana 64   Purdue 41

Assembly Hall

March 3, 1983

I t was a Bob Knight-kind of team. Senior-smart. Senior-experienced. Senior-poised.

Then it took a devastating hit. And that's when it proved it truly was a Bob Knight-kind of college basketball team.

Knight occasionally went for size, with 7-foot-2 sophomore Uwe Blab at center. Sometimes he added backcourt quickness with freshman Stew Robinson, or

Five-year friends and team leaders Randy Wittman and Ted Kitchel went out with a banner year.

No.		Height	Class	G-S	Pts.
30	Ted Kitchel*	6-8	Sr.	24-23	17.3
20	Jim Thomas	6-3	Sr.	30-28	10.2
33	Uwe Blab	7-2	So.	30-19	9.4
24	Randy Wittman*	6-6	Sr.	30-30	18.9
31	Tony Brown	6-2	Sr.	29-18	5.2
54	Steve Bouchie	6-8	Sr.	30-15	6.3
21	Winston Morgan	6-5	So.	27-5	2.9
22	Stew Robinson	6-1	Fr.	26-9	1.9
11	Dan Dakich	6-5	So.	17-1	1.6
25	Cam Cameron	6-2	Sr.	15-0	0.5
41	Mike Giomi	6-9	Fr.	19-0	2.3
42	John Flowers	6-9	So.	8-2	3.3
40	Tracy Foster	6-4	Fr.	2-0	0.0

Wittman: Basketball Writers All-America, Big Ten MVP, All-Big Ten; Kitchel: All-Big Ten.

athletic strength with sophomore Winston Morgan.

Most of the time, in the biggest of times, five seniors did the job for Indiana, did it so well they spent some time No. 1-ranked in the land.

The leaders were Ted Kitchel and Randy Wittman, five-year roommates and superb shooters in a season when the Big Ten experimented with a 3-point shot line.

The Hoosiers blew through their pre-league opponents 10-0 to rise to No. 1 ranking. Then they opened Big Ten play at Ohio State and lost, 70-67. The only official 3-point try for Indiana that night was just ahead of the buzzer, and it was by Tony Brown — another of those senior starters, along with Steve Bouchie and Jim Thomas.

Indiana went from there to Illinois. Knight set up an offense with Kitchel in one corner and Wittman in the other. Illinois opened in a zone defense. Kitchel shot over it and hit. Twice. So did Wittman. Nothing

Winston Morgan takes the high way to two.

24-6; Big Ten 13-5, Champion

Ball State	W	91-75
at Miami, Ohio	W	75-59
Texas-El Paso	W	65-54
at Notre Dame	W	68-52
Eastern Michigan [1]	W	85-48
Wyoming [1]	W	78-65
at Kansas State	W	48-46
Kentucky	W	62-59
Grambling [2]	W	110-62
Nebraska [2]	W	67-50
at Ohio State	L	67-70
at Illinois	W	69-55
at Purdue	W	81-78
Michigan State	W	89-85
Michigan	W	93-76
at Northwestern	W	78-73
at Iowa	L	48-63
Wisconsin	W	83-73
Minnesota	W	76-51
at Minnesota	W	63-59
at Wisconsin	W	75-56
Iowa	L	57-58
Northwestern	W	74-65
at Michigan	L	56-69
at Michigan State	L	54-62
Purdue	W	64-41
Illinois	W	67-55
Ohio State	W	81-60

N	C	A	A
Oklahoma [3]		W	63-49
Kentucky [4]		L	59-64

[1] *Indiana Classic*
[2] *Hoosier Classic, Indianapolis*
[3] *at Evansville, Indiana*
[4] *at Knoxville, Tennessee*

new there, Illini coach Lou Henson said, "Indiana just may be the best zone offense team in the country."

The two combined for 47 points and Indiana got its slightly belated first league victory, 69-55.

Wittman had 27 of those points. Wittman was an old familiar player with an all-new look. Reluctant to shoot most of his career, he stepped forward as a co-leader of the Hoosier offense with Kitchel, who never had to fight a shooting reluctance.

Wittman came out firing. In the opener against Ball State, he hit 12 of a career-high 20 shots, scored 28 points and blanketed Ball State scoring star (now coach) Ray McCallum. At Miami of Ohio, Wittman was 15-for-21 with 31 points. "He's just a great player," Miami coach Darrell Hedric said, "an All-American."

In seven games their senior season, both Kitchel and Wittman scored in the 20s. Among Knight-era duos, Scott May and Kent Benson did it nine times in The Perfect Season, Mike Woodson and Wayne Radford seven times in 1978-79, but those were over a full season, including post-season.

The Kitchel-Wittman act didn't play that long. With the Hoosiers surging along at 20-3, two games ahead in the Big Ten at 10-3, they played at Michigan Feb. 24 and Kitchel's career ended. Six minutes into the game, Kitchel sank his last Indiana shot – ironically, a 3-pointer – and seconds later left with intense back pains. Back surgery ended his season.

Indiana lost that game, 69-56. The Hoosiers moved on to Michigan State and lost again, 62-54. Their lead was gone, Ohio State and Purdue pulling even.

Indiana (10-5) was left with three games at home: with Purdue (10-5), Illinois (8-6) and Ohio State (10-5).

"When your star gets hurt, naturally your other guys get fired up," Purdue's third-year coach, Gene Keady, said. That was after Indiana's stunning 64-41 rout that opened the homestretch run, after the Hoosiers – sent into play with roaring support from the 17,312 at Assembly Hall – tore into Purdue for a 6-0 jumpout that became 12-2, then 28-12.

Ted Kitchel is on guard against Iowa's Craig Anderson.

Keady said the Hoosiers "did a great job of going back to their early days of ball control and tight defense. They were a very good basketball team tonight. They ought to be league champions, if they keep it up."

Keeping it up was uppermost in Knight's mind, too. Over the years he had been critical of the blase nature of Assembly Hall crowds. This one arrived with foxhole intensity. It was into an electric pre-game roar, just before tipoff, when Kitchel came out of the dressing room and slowly, carefully, firmly walked to the Indiana bench. When he popped through into general view and was recognized, the noise escalated with emotional applause, long and loud seconds of it.

Kitchel's surprise appearance was an ace the Hoosiers used up with this game. The emotion of the crowd was another. Knight wanted to make sure the latter didn't ebb. Before leaving the floor, he picked up the courtside microphone and told the crowd: "We need you Saturday night, too."

It was there (17,328), and Illinois, fresh from a 74-73 victory over Ohio State that dealt the Illini into the race, caught a 67-55 blast. Ohio State won at Purdue, so only the Buckeyes were left in catching range on the last day of the season. One more time the crowd (17,343) was wild. One more time the Hoosiers reacted with a game-opening pounce: 7-2, then 19-5, then a startling 32-12 on the way to 42-22 at halftime. The second-half margin topped at 29 before the final 81-60 score.

Wittman, so far off his game the first night he played (at Michigan State) after Kitchel's injury, had 24 points against Ohio State, 60 in those low-scoring, high-volume last three games – 26-for-45 shooting (.578) with everything on the line. Knight pronounced him the obvious Big Ten MVP, and it came to pass.

But Knight also had a Senior Day tribute for that stretch-run "sixth man" who was not graduating. He promised the crowd: "We've always kinda reserved banners in here for things that happened on a national level. We're going to break from that tradition a little bit. Because everybody had a big part in this, when you come in here next fall, down there (pointing to the north end) there will be a banner that says '1983 Big Ten Champions.'

"Remember when you see it, that's a banner that belongs to every one of you."

Randy Wittman began his All-America senior season at top speed and kept it up.

Indiana 72   North Carolina 68

The Omni   Atlanta, Georgia

March 22, 1984

Bob Knight spends some Olympic Trials time with close friend Pete Newell, his predecessor as a coach of champions in the NCAA tournament, NIT and Olympic Games.

It was a year that started as none ever had in the 13-year Bob Knight coaching era at Indiana: with a home-court loss.

Miami of Ohio, with a future NBA player in Ron Harper and a long history of upset victims in both football and basketball, jolted the Hoosiers on opening day, 73-67, with 26 points from Harper.

Knight hadn't started freshmen Steve Alford and Marty Simmons that day, but he played them more than anyone else: 31 minutes for Alford (who scored 12 points) and 33 for Simmons (15).

Each was a regular from there on, a year that stretched into the summer for rookie Alford and saw him start – with, among others, Michael Jordan and Patrick Ewing – on the gold-medal team Knight coached at the Los Angeles Olympics.

Maybe the freshman prominence had something to do with it, but it was a year of more than usual Hoosier volatility. Up in playing No. 1-ranked Kentucky to a 59-54 scrape at Lexington. Down in losing at Texas-El Paso, 65-61. Up in jumping out 2-0 in the Big Ten by winning at Ohio State, then in overtime at home over No. 9-ranked Illinois. Down in spoiling that start by giving up 22 straight points, wrapped around halftime, in a 74-66 loss to Purdue. Up in breathing life back into their Big Ten hopes with a 78-59 shocker at No. 9-ranked Purdue. Back down, and out of the league race, in a 70-53 wipeout three days later at Illinois.

No.		Height	Class	G-S	Pts.
51	Marty Simmons	6-5	Fr.	31-26	9.4
41	Mike Giomi	6-9	So.	27-15	8.7
33	Uwe Blab	7-2	Jr.	31-27	11.8
12	Steve Alford	6-2	Fr.	31-27	15.5
22	Stew Robinson	6-1	So.	30-15	7.9
23	Chuck Franz	6-2	Sr.	27-10	3.7
11	Dan Dakich	6-5	Jr.	24-4	3.9
30	Todd Meier	6-8	Fr.	26-7	2.9
24	Daryl Thomas	6-7	Fr.	25-6	2.8
21	Winston Morgan*	6-5	Jr.	6-2	6.7
52	Courtney Witte	6-8	Jr.	20-1	0.9
40	Tracy Foster	6-4	So.	6-0	2.7

* Injury, red-shirted

Marty Simmons, finding passing room, and Steve Alford found prominent roles as freshmen.

Daryl Thomas squeezes a rebound against Wisconsin.

The Hoosiers were an unexciting 20-8 invitee in the 53-team NCAA tournament. They expected to meet Charles Barkley, Chuck Person and Auburn after a first-round bye, but Richmond took out Auburn and Indiana hurdled the Spiders, 75-67.

The Hoosiers' reward: advancement to the Sweet 16 against No. 1-ranked North Carolina and College Player of the Year, Michael Jordan.

When the Hoosiers reassembled in Bloomington the day after beating Richmond in Charlotte, Knight opened his lockerroom talk with them: "We're going to beat North Carolina, and here's how it's going to be done." Everything from that moment on was positive about the victory that was going to happen, and how.

The night before the game, in his Atlanta hotel room, Knight went around the room with his coaching staff soliciting lineup opinions. When it got to Knight, he mentioned a name that hadn't come up with any of the others. Dan Dakich.

Then Knight went to an adjoining room where the players were gathered. He made them laugh with a comic opening line, then talked confidently one more time about what was going to happen the next day. He gave out the lineup by listing defensive assignments.

Dakich on Jordan.

"I went back to my room and threw up," Dakich said/joked/admitted later.

Dakich had played key roles in some big victories, usually as a substitute. When Indiana came from 15 points behind to beat Minnesota, 74-72, despite .714 shooting by the Gophers, Knight credited the victory to sub Dakich for a variety of contributions. But he stayed a reserve. His start against North Carolina was just his sixth of the year, and he averaged just over 10 minutes a game.

Jordan scored the game's first two baskets. Dakich's primary responsibilities were to take away the drive and to deny North Carolina a favorite weapon: lobs to Jordan around the basket. If that meant jump-shot openings, fine. The Jordan of 1984 was brilliantly skilled but not the shooter he was to become after, as a pro, blossoming into the greatest player the game has seen.

Jordan's second foul came on one of those attempted Alley Oops, when he was called for jumping into Dakich. That was with 12:45 left in the half, Indiana up 10-8, and coach Dean Smith pulled him. It was a move common to both Smith and Knight: making sure a key player opens the second half with no more than two fouls. Indiana went to the lockerroom up 32-28, and Jordan returned to start the second half.

North Carolina never did catch up.

Jordan converted an Indiana turnover into a basket in the third minute of the second half, then, five seconds apart, drew Dakich's third and fourth fouls. But Dakich stayed in and Jordan never scored again till a dunk with five minutes left, on a turnover conversion.

By then, No. 1 was on the Hoosier hook. When Alford stole the ball and sped to a layup with 5:39 left, Indiana led 59-47 and CBS announcer Billy Packer told the national viewing audience, "This game is over."

It wasn't. In a 38-second stretch, rookie Simmons missed three one-and-one chances, Chuck Franz another. The first of those Simmons chances came on Jordan's fourth foul, but also in that stretch, Jordan had that dunk, then another basket and a free throw (Dakich's fifth foul) and North Carolina was within 59-57 with 3:25 to play.

Alford, the national free-throw champion that year at .917, steadied the Hoosiers with a one-and-one conversion with 3:12 to play. Jordan's last college basket put North Carolina within 62-60, but the Tar Heels again fouled Alford (one-and-one, making it 64-60, 1:59 left). When Jordan missed a shot, Alford rebounded and he was knocked to the floor. When an official signaled he had been fouled, Alford, still down, shot a jaunty arm into the air. He, a freshman, would get to shoot the critical one-and-one. And again he hit both to open the lead to 66-60 with 1:42 left.

Half-a-minute later, Jordan drew his fifth foul.

Still, it was 68-66 with 19 seconds left when North Carolina intentionally fouled Blab, a .620 free-throw shooter. "I'm always confident it's going in," Blab had said of his free-throw stroke. "Sometimes I get fooled. Sometimes I get *really* fooled."

This time he hit both. The Hoosiers let 12 free-throw points slip away in the final five minutes but delivered the victory Knight had all but promised them.

Smith was crushed but gracious. Alford, he said, "doesn't look like a freshman guard, does he? He sure shot it." Alford hit 9 of 13 shots, 9 of 10 free throws, and scored 27 points, to 13 for Jordan (6-for-14 in 26 minutes) and 26 for Sam Perkins, his future Olympic teammates.

Smith added one more thing: "Dakich played great defense."

Two days later, actually about 38 hours later, 11-game loser Virginia brought the Hoosiers down, 50-48, and advanced to the Final Four.

The 72-68 game — and its major players: Jordan-defender Dakich, rookie executioner Alford, victory designer Knight — survived the letdown and became a special part of Hoosier legendry.

Uwe Blab, a 7-foot-2 Phi Beta

Kappan, claims a rebound.

1 9 8 3 – 1 9 8 4		
22-9; Big Ten 13-5, Third		
Miami, Ohio	L	57-63
Notre Dame	W	80-72
at Kentucky	L	54-59
Tennessee Tech	W	81-66
at Texas-El Paso	L	61-65
Texas A&M [1]	W	73-48
Illinois State [1]	W	54-44
Kansas State	*W	56-53
Ball State [2]	W	86-43
Boston College [2]	W	72-66
at Ohio State	W	73-62
Illinois	*W	73-68
Purdue	L	66-74
at Michigan State	*W	70-62
at Michigan	L	50-55
Northwestern	W	57-44
Iowa	W	54-47
at Minnesota	W	67-54
at Wisconsin	W	81-67
Wisconsin	W	74-64
Minnesota	*W	74-72
at Iowa	W	49-45
at Northwestern	L	51-63
Michigan	W	72-57
Michigan State	L	54-57
at Purdue	W	78-59
at Illinois	L	53-70
Ohio State	W	53-49
N C A A		
Richmond [3]	W	75-67
North Carolina [4]	W	72-68
Virginia [4]	L	48-50

* *Overtime*
[1] *Indiana Classic*
[2] *Hoosier Classic, Indianapolis*
[3] *at Charlotte, North Carolina*
[4] *at Atlanta, Georgia*

Indiana 87   Michigan 62

Crisler Arena   Ann Arbor, Michigan

January 2, 1985

Golfshirt-clad Bob Knight's call for a held-ball ruling went unmet against Purdue.

In Indiana basketball history, in Bob Knight history, 1984–85 always will be The Year of The Chair.

Actually, it was two years, two distinctly different seasons that became the longest year – and not just figuratively – in Knight's career.

It began as soon as the 1983-84 season ended at Atlanta. Instantly, Indiana Coach Knight converted to U.S.

Olympic Coach Knight, the latter a role he had been squeezing in every time he could since his appointment to the job in May 1982. He went to the 1984 Final Four in Seattle and completed the 74-man invitation list for the U.S. Trials, held in Bloomington in April. The 16 finalists for the team were brought back to Bloomington in late-May. In June, the team began an exhibition tour, including a game at Assembly Hall against former IU stars. In early July, the Olympians christened the new Hoosier Dome in Indianapolis by bringing in 67,596 people – a record for basketball in the U.S. – to see an exhibition game against an NBA All-Star team led by Larry Bird and former Hoosier Isiah Thomas. Then came the rest of a cross-country tour, before the Games in Los Angeles, capped by a 96-65 gold-medal victory over Spain on Aug. 10.

And then, after only a too-brief break, there was basketball again.

The Chair incident overshadowed everything in the

No.		Height	Class	G-S	Pts.
32	Steve Eyl	6-6	Fr.	29-14	4.8
11	Dan Dakich	6-5	Sr.	28-11	5.2
33	Uwe Blab	7-2	Sr.	33-31	16.0
12	Steve Alford	6-2	So.	32-31	18.1
22	Stew Robinson	6-1	Jr.	29-14	6.1
24	Daryl Thomas	6-7	So.	21-10	5.5
21	Winston Morgan	6-5	Jr.	21-11	5.2
23	Delray Brooks	6-4	Fr.	32-12	3.6
51	Marty Simmons	6-5	So.	23-9	3.7
30	Todd Meier	6-8	So.	30-8	2.6
42	Kreigh Smith	6-7	Fr.	23-1	3.1
44	Joe Hillman	6-2	Fr.	21-1	1.5
45	Brian Sloan	6-8	Fr.	17-1	0.8
14	Magnus Pelkowski	6-10	Fr.	15-0	0.9
41	Mike Giomi	6-8	Jr.	15-11	9.5

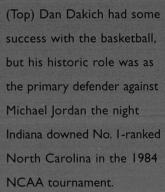

(Top) Dan Dakich had some success with the basketball, but his historic role was as the primary defender against Michael Jordan the night Indiana downed No. 1-ranked North Carolina in the 1984 NCAA tournament.

(Bottom) Delray Brooks, now a Rick Pitino assistant at Kentucky, plays against the Blue in an 81-68 Indiana victory.

19-14 season. It came early in a Feb. 23 home-court loss to Purdue. Knight objected to a foul call on a play in front of his bench, then again on another involving the pass-in from the same area. He drew a technical foul, escalating his exasperation. He fumed on, long enough for Purdue guard Steve Reid to go to the free-throw line to shoot the technical free throws, then grabbed a courtside chair, probably his own, and sent it spinning onto the court. It brought him expulsion and a one-game Big Ten suspension, plus a special notoriety that is unending.

Knight had spent his first 19½ years as a head coach wearing a dress shirt and tie, and wondering why. In the Olympics he had worn a golf shirt. That day against Purdue, he had changed attire and gone onto the court wearing a mostly white golf shirt with thin red horizontal stripes. He was no stranger to throwing things when angry, usually the sports coat he was wearing or had just shed, sometimes a clipboard – always down, never out, onto the court. This day, there was no coat to throw. This time, the first loose thing his eyes picked up was the chair, and his career took on a signature symbol – by no means his angriest outburst but, apparently, judging by its frequency of replay over the years, his most singular and photogenic. More than a decade later, Knight and chair are word-association couplings.

He hasn't coached in a coat and tie since. A sweater, over a golf shirt, became his attire of identity. But The Chair only typified the longest and hardest two months

of Knight's years at Indiana. In a 50-day, 14-game stretch, Indiana lost 10 times. An unimaginable five straight losses came at Assembly Hall, where other than that year Indiana losses have averaged barely over one per season (30 in 24 years, going into 1996-97). The Chair game was the third loss of the five-game Assembly Hall streak, the seventh of the 10 defeats in the 14-game tailspin. In there were a game at Illinois where he sat down all upperclassmen but center Blab, and dismissal of team rebounding leader Mike Giomi for missing classes, a generally stormy stretch in which Knight, for a rare time in his coaching career, couldn't find the motivational pieces to get his team winning.

What came before that offered few hints. The Hoosiers were 11-3. They lost their season opener at home to Louisville – the last home game an Indiana team was to lose to a non-Big Ten team for more than 11 years – but that was to a group that would win the 1986 NCAA championship. The 1984-85 Hoosiers

(Above right) The launch that never dies – Bob Knight gets set to send a sideline chair onto the court and himself into infamy against Purdue.

(Right) An Olympic carryover in the Assembly Hall stands, after Los Angeles.

had some outstanding early victories – over Kentucky (81-68, shooting .661); at Kansas State (70-58 over a 6-0 Wildcat team, Steve Alford scoring 32 points); in the finals of the Hoosier Classic at Indianapolis over 7-0 Florida (80-63, when senior Dan Dakich made a run at the first triple-double in IU history with 23 points, 10 rebounds and 7 assists).

Knight's team made an impressive start in Big Ten play at Ann Arbor, against a veteran, talented Michigan team that was ranked in the Top 20 and expected to make a run at the Big Ten championship, and did.

The Wolverines – future longtime pros Roy Tarpley and Gary Grant, plus Antoine Joubert, Richard Rellford and Butch Wade – didn't just win the Big Ten championship, they went 16-2 and closed with a 15-game winning streak.

The '84-85 Hoosiers, who finished 7-11 in Big Ten play, came out of that opening night at Crisler Arena with an 87-62 victory, a record winning margin for a Crisler visitor.

Blab, dominating Tarpley, had 19 points by halftime, and Indiana led, 43-37. Grant had been neutralizing Alford up to then. Alford didn't miss a shot in a 12-point second half that lifted him to 19 for the game, 10 of those points in a stunning Hoosier pullaway from 53-48 to 68-50 on the way to 80-52. In that 27-4 blitz, the Hoosiers hit 13 straight shots. Blab finished with 31 points, 13-for-17 from the field, 7-for-8 on hook shots.

(Left) Uwe Blab's hook shot started way up there.

(Bottom left) Joe Hillman and seniors Dan Dakich and Uwe Blab check out the NIT runnerup trophy after a 65-62 final-game loss to UCLA and Reggie Miller.

Indiana's .667 shooting for the game was the third-best in school history for a conference game.

Three nights later, the Hoosiers lost at Michigan State, 68-61. Their slide began just three games later. Alford, the youngest 1984 Olympian and that great team's shooting leader at .644, was shooting .633 for his sophomore season when he left Ann Arbor. In the team's late-season nosedive, he went 2-for-12 in one game and 17-for-63 (.270) over a five-game stretch.

Alford finally threw that off when Michigan and Indiana met again, on the last day of the regular season at Assembly Hall. Alford was 11-for-16 for 22 points, Blab scored 23, but Grant picked up a deflection and scored just ahead of the buzzer for a 73-71 Michigan victory.

Alford went on to shoot just under .600 and average 21.6 in leading the Hoosiers past Butler, Richmond, Marquette and Tennessee to the championship game of the NIT. The title got away, 65-62, to UCLA, which got 18 points on 9-for-14 long-range bombing by tournament MVP Reggie Miller, a sophomore. "Miller," Knight said afterward, "is a *very* good shooter."

19-14; Big Ten 7-11, Seventh

Louisville	L	64-75
Ohio	W	90-73
at Notre Dame	L	63-74
Kentucky	W	81-68
at Iowa State	W	69-67
Western Kentucky [1]	W	80-57
St. Joseph's, Pa. [1]	W	81-44
at Kansas State	W	70-58
Miami, Ohio [2]	W	77-72
Florida [2]	W	80-63
at Michigan	W	87-62
at Michigan State	L	61-68
Northwestern	W	77-50
Wisconsin	W	90-68
at Ohio State	L	84-86
at Purdue	L	52-62
at Illinois	L	41-52
Iowa	L	59-72
Minnesota	W	89-66
at Wisconsin	W	58-54
at Northwestern	W	78-59
Ohio State	L	63-72
Illinois	L	50-66
Purdue	L	63-72
at Minnesota	W	79-68
at Iowa	L	50-70
Michigan State	L	58-68
Michigan	L	71-73
N	I	T
Butler [3]	W	79-57
Richmond [3]	W	75-53
Marquette [3]	**W	94-82
Tennessee [4]	W	74-67
UCLA [4]	L	62-65

**Double Overtime
[1] *Indiana Classic*
[2] *Hoosier Classic, Indianapolis*
[3] *at Assembly Hall*
[4] *at New York*

89

Indiana 12-6
Canada, Japan, China, Yugoslavia & Finland
Summer 1985

(Left) At Ohio State, Bob Knight's nickname was 'Dragon;' on tour in China, 'Dragon' met dragon.

(Right) The Great Wall of China was the highlight of a 37-day, 11-nation tour for many of Indiana's basketball travelers, including (from left) Brian Sloan, Todd Meier, Steve Eyl, coach Bob Knight, Tim Knight, Kreigh Smith, assistant coach Kohn Smith, and Magnus Pelkowski.

Indiana, with its 1984 U.S. Olympic coach, Bob Knight, was invited to represent United States basketball in the four-nation Kirin World Basketball championships in Japan in early-summer 1985.

The Hoosiers were coming off their toughest season of the 25 Knight years: 7-11 in the Big Ten, a five-game home-court losing streak at one stretch. Knight saw the trip as a chance to squeeze in some extra bonding time for a team that had struggled.

So he didn't just accept the Japan trip but grafted onto it before and after for what turned into an 18-game, 37-day, 11-nation trip.

The Hoosiers played in five nations: Canada, Japan, China, Yugoslavia and Finland. They also had a three-day stop in Hong Kong and an overnight in Amsterdam. They spent a half-day at the Great Wall of China, at a point about an hour north of Beijing. They visited the Ming Tombs, the shrines at Kyoto. They played the Japan National team in Hiroshima on July 4, as part of the Kirin Tournament, and the same team the next day in Nagasaki – when demonstrations already were starting to take shape for the 40th anniversary of the atomic bombings, marked a month later.

On their return, senior guard Winston Morgan said of all the sights seen on the five-week tour, "the Wall – that's got to be the most unbelievable thing."

Sophomore Joe Hillman agreed. "In Japan, it was Hiroshima, but the Wall has to be the greatest thing, without a doubt."

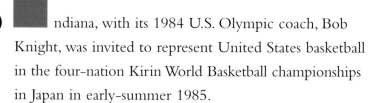

No.		Height	Class	G-S	Pts.
12	Steve Alford	6-2	Jr.	16-15	17.4
24	Daryl Thomas	6-7	Jr.	18-17	10.9
22	Stew Robinson	6-1	Sr.	14-10	8.6
21	Winston Morgan	6-5	Sr.	18-13	8.4
32	Steve Eyl	6-6	So.	18-13	7.2
44	Joe Hillman	6-2	So.	18-5	6.9
23	Delray Brooks	6-4	So.	17-4	6.1
45	Brian Sloan	6-8	So.	18-2	4.6
30	Todd Meier	6-8	Jr.	18-2	4.4
42	Kreigh Smith	6-7	So.	17-0	2.5
14	Magnus Pelkowski	6-10	So.	16-9	2.3

Japan's 7-foot-9 center, Chibi Okayama, gave a merry sendoff to Stew Robinson (6-1) and Winston Morgan (6-4) after the Hoosiers' seven games in the Kirin World tour.

Junior Daryl Thomas, in a diary kept on the trip, said: "I got a weird feeling (from visiting the Atomic Bomb site and peace park at Hiroshima). Just going through and seeing the things you see makes me wonder what it would be like if the bomb went off today. *The Day After* (a movie) made me stop and think, but the Atomic Bomb Memorial – that's reality."

The Hoosiers, of course, also played basketball. They lost six of their first eight games, two of those by

20 points each to the Soviet Union National team that had skipped the Los Angeles Olympics. Both Knight and Olympian Steve Alford made it clear they didn't feel the Soviets would have changed the gold-medal outcome if they had gone to Los Angeles. "We'd have killed them," Alford said. "There's no way those guys would have stopped Michael (Jordan), Sam Perkins, Patrick Ewing – not as careless as the Russians are."

Knight made his point puckishly. In the traditional pre-game exchange of gifts with Soviet coach Vladimir Obhov at Kobe, Knight – with a package flown over by request from Nike, just out with the product – gave Obhov "Air Jordan" shoes as a reminder of what he had missed by not playing at Los Angeles.

The Hoosiers won their last 10 games on the trip, and it was during that stretch that Knight experimented with the 6-7 Thomas as a center. The experiment carried over into the 1985-86 season and was a key to that team's improvement.

Knight took along on the trip two 80-plus coaching giants: Everett Dean, Indiana's first All-America player and coach of the Hoosiers from 1925 to '38, and Henry Iba, coach of two NCAA champions at Oklahoma A&M and three U.S. Olympic teams.

Iba said "The Great Wall was wonderful, but to me the greatest thing was the way this team came around. That to me isn't the bottom line. That's the top line."

CANADA		
At Toronto		
Canada National	W	82-75
At Hamilton		
Canada National	L	85-101

JAPAN		
At Tokyo		
Japan National	W	72-59
USSR National	L	54-74
At Hiroshima		
Japan National	L	59-68
At Nagasaki		
Japan National	L	67-74
At Kumamoto		
Netherlands National	L	49-67
At Kobe		
USSR National	L	71-91
At Sapporo		
Netherlands National	W	82-69

91

CHINA		
At Beijing		
China National	W	73-71
At Nanjing		
Jiangsu Province	W	79-59
At Beijing		
Shanghai	W	102-76

YUGOSLAVIA		
At Pozarevac		
Yugoslavia Junior	W	76-72
At Obrenovac		
Yugoslavia Junior	W	66-59
At Obrenovac		
Yugoslavia Junior	W	73-62

FINLAND		
At Kotka		
Finland National	W	92-83
At Salo		
Finland National	W	91-84
At Helsinki		
Finland National	W	88-74

Indiana 97   Michigan State 79

Jenison Fieldhouse   East Lansing, Michigan

March 5, 1986

Answers from anywhere would be welcomed by Bob Knight.

o Indiana basketball team ever traveled farther to get itself into a Big Ten championship race than the 1985-86 Hoosiers.

This was the Indiana season that was described in a national best-seller, *Washington Post* sportswriter John Feinstein's *Season on the Brink*. It turned out to be the season that was on the brink of a national-championship year for Indiana.

But this Indiana team was coming back from a 7-11

No.		Height	Class	G-S	Pts.
20	Ricky Calloway	6-6	Fr.	29-27	13.9
34	Andre Harris	6-6	Jr.	29-25	8.4
24	Daryl Thomas	6-7	Jr.	26-26	14.5
12	Steve Alford*	6-2	Jr.	28-28	22.5
21	Winston Morgan	6-5	Sr.	29-21	6.6
22	Stew Robinson	6-1	Sr.	28-8	5.9
23	Delray Brooks	6-4	So.	11-1	2.4
32	Steve Eyl	6-6	So.	27-1	1.5
11	Todd Jadlow	6-9	Jr.	22-2	2.6
30	Todd Meier	6-8	Jr.	25-3	1.7
52	Courtney Witte	6-8	Sr.	14-1	1.6
42	Kreigh Smith*	6-7	So.	3-1	4.0

* Alford: Consensus All-America, All-Big Ten; Smith: injured, red-shirted.

Big Ten finish. A considerable climb was needed from there to title contention, and the Hoosiers started in that direction as circuitously as could be imagined. They spent more than seven weeks of their summer on an 18-game, round-the-world trip – to Canada, Japan, China, Hong Kong, Yugoslavia and Finland, with stops in Hiroshima and Nagasaki, visits to the Great Wall and the Ming Tombs, overnights in San Francisco and Amsterdam.

The bonding and the basketball growth intended as by-products of the traveling first surfaced in a 10-game winning streak closing out the trip.

No player grew more than junior Daryl Thomas, who showed Knight, his teammates and himself that – at 6-7 – he could be a solid collegiate center.

The move radically changed the Hoosier look from the four seasons with 7-2 Uwe Blab in that spot. The size Thomas gave away was offset by considerably more mobility. Opening day, Thomas had 15 points but an eye-catching six steals, two of them in a late-game stretch

Daryl Thomas had to play
out of position at center but
made it work against Illinois,
and lots of others.

Winston Morgan's defensive job wasn't easy against Big Ten scoring champion Scott Skiles of Michigan State.

that changed a 55-54 lead over Kent State to 69-56 on the way to an 89-73 victory.

Thomas became so valuable for the Hoosiers that when he missed a game, it was critical. An ankle sprain in practice the day before made him sit out a 77-74 home-court loss to Michigan State the opening weekend of the Big Ten season. The loss plunged the Hoosiers into an immediate 0-2 league start – both of them home games (the first 74-69 to reigning champion and league favorite Michigan).

From that beginning, the Hoosiers outplayed every other team in the league, going 12-2 over the next seven weeks. But the extra penalty for the home-court losses opening the season was that the same two teams had to be met, on the road, in the weekend closing out the year.

Michigan State had become a third Big Ten power. Native Hoosier Scott Skiles of Plymouth's 1982 state high school champions was the league's scoring leader, averaging more than 28 points a game.

The Spartans' key was shooting – .564 for the season when Indiana arrived at Jenison Fieldhouse, where Michigan State had shot .594, .661, .625 and .627 in its last four home games. And the Spartans had swept both games from Michigan, so Indiana and Michigan went into that final week 12-4 in the league, Michigan State 11-5.

Rarely has a game plan worked out more precisely on-court than the Hoosiers' dissection of the trademark Jud Heathcote zone defense. This Spartan zone,

94

A rallying moment always saved for the final minutes at Assembly Hall, a banner-waving end to the pep band version of "1812 Overture."

Knight told his players with film, blackboard and live demonstration, could be beaten by quick player and ball movement setting up three-on-two or two-on-one advantages — and taking immediate advantage. The Hoosiers did it to spring Steve Alford for 31 points, freshman Rick Calloway for 19, Thomas for 14.

This night it was Indiana that shot .614, and Michigan State which seemed almost chilly at .508. "We live by our free throws and our field-goal shooting," Skiles said. "We're not as good a team when we're missing. But it wasn't so much our missed free throws (19-for-30) as our lack of defense tonight."

Wire to wire it was Indiana — after a 7-2 spot at the start, anyway. The Hoosiers led 48-35 at halftime, despite 21 points by Skiles; 97-79 at game's end, Skiles finishing with 33.

"Maybe I should give Indiana more credit than I feel like doing," Heathcote said. "We played so poorly that we made them look good. But maybe they played so well they made us look bad."

Alford could only reflect on a year's difference. "We had to go through last season," he said. "We lose so many at home, so many period…we go to the NIT, we don't get accepted to the NCAA when the largest field in NCAA history starts…I think that's what's the most pleasing. We've made a complete turn-around from last year."

Knight talked of "major contributions from everybody," including Thomas who "played down to the wire well with four fouls. And I thought Steve played extremely well."

The Hoosiers' comeback season crested there. They went on to Michigan and caught a Senior Day blast from the veteran Wolverines, 80-52, to decide the league championship. Six days later, in Round 1 of the NCAA tournament, the 21-8 season ended with an 83-79 loss to underrated and greatly underseeded Cleveland State at Syracuse. Meanwhile, the Michigan team that looked so overpowering against Indiana lost in the tournament's second round to Iowa State and longtime Wolverine coach Johnny Orr. Among Big Ten teams, it was Michigan State that went the farthest, beating Washington and Georgetown before being tripped up by late-game clock trouble in an overtime Sweet 16 loss to Kansas at Kansas City.

Not nice, but not wrong,
often, at Assembly Hall.

1985 – 1986		
21-8; Big Ten 13-5, Second		
Kent State	W	89-73
Notre Dame	W	82-67
at Kentucky	L	58-63
Kansas State	W	78-71
Louisiana Tech [1]	W	84-63
Texas Tech [1]	W	74-59
at Louisville	L	63-65
Iowa State	W	86-65
Idaho [2]	W	87-57
Mississippi State [2]	W	74-43
Michigan	L	69-74
Michigan State	L	74-77
at Northwestern	W	102-65
at Wisconsin	W	80-69
Ohio State	W	69-66
Purdue	*W	71-70
Illinois	W	71-69
at Iowa	L	69-79
at Minnesota	W	62-54
Wisconsin	W	78-69
Northwestern	W	77-52
at Ohio State	W	84-75
at Illinois	W	61-60
at Purdue	L	68-85
Minnesota	W	95-63
Iowa	W	80-73
at Michigan State	W	97-79
at Michigan	L	52-80
N C A A		
Cleveland State [3]	L	79-83

* *Overtime*
[1] *Indiana Classic*
[2] *Hoosier Classic, Indianapolis*
[3] *at Syracuse, New York*

Indiana 86 Wisconsin 85 Triple Overtime

Wisconsin Fieldhouse Madison, Wisconsin

February 16, 1987

(Left) Bob Knight enjoys a tournament-time laugh with a member of his 1984 Olympic staff, C.M. Newton.

(Right) Keith Smart burst into national prominence in the NCAA tournament.

In modern college basketball, North Carolina State (1983) and Villanova (1985) generally are considered the NCAA tournament's longshot champions.

By at least one criterion, Indiana (1987) beats them all.

The National Basketball Assn. celebrated its 50th season in 1996-97. In that half-century, no other team won an NCAA championship with as little NBA-certified

No.		Height	Class	G-S	Pts.
24	Daryl Thomas	6-7	Sr.	34-34	15.7
20	Ricky Calloway	6-6	So.	29-27	12.6
22	Dean Garrett	6-10	Jr.	34-33	11.4
12	Steve Alford*	6-2	Sr.	34-34	22.0
23	Keith Smart*	6-1	Jr.	34-31	11.2
32	Steve Eyl	6-6	Jr.	34-1	3.0
30	Todd Meier	6-8	Sr.	29-0	1.1
44	Joe Hillman	6-2	So.	32-5	2.5
45	Brian Sloan	6-8	So.	17-1	2.1
14	Magnus Pelkowski	6-10	So.	14-1	3.8
42	Kreigh Smith	6-7	So.	25-1	1.5
10	Tony Freeman	5-7	Fr.	16-0	2.2
35	Jeff Oliphant	6-5	So.	2-0	1.5
31	Dave Minor	6-5	Fr.	18-2	0.8

* Alford: Consensus All-America, All-Big Ten, Big Ten MVP, Big Ten Athlete of Year, All-Final Four; Smart: Outstanding Player Award, Final Four.

"talent" as the 1986-87 Hoosiers.

Only three other teams in that entire era did it without a future NBA first-round draft pick in a major role – Loyola in '63, Kentucky in '58 and, ironically, Indiana in '53. The NBA was considerably smaller in those years. Loyola's Jerry Harkness was the first player taken in the second round of the '63 NBA draft, No. 10 overall. Kentucky's Vern Hatton went No. 2 on Round 2 in the '58 NBA draft, the 10th player taken overall. Both Bob Leonard and Dick Farley, junior stars for the '53 Hoosiers, were second-round picks in the nine-team NBA's 1954 draft and went on to solid NBA careers – brief in the case of Farley, who helped Syracuse to the 1955 NBA championship but retired early and was just 37 when he died of cancer in 1969.

The '87 Hoosiers' best player, Olympian and two-year All-American Steve Alford, went third in the second round of the '87 draft, No. 26 overall. Three other Hoosier regulars – Keith Smart, Rick Calloway and

High school quarterback
Steve Eyl never was one
to pass up a dunk.

Dean Garrett – each played at least a little in the NBA, Garrett not till his ninth post-college year after a good career in Europe. All the '87 Hoosiers together haven't combined for 1,000 career NBA points.

But time and time and time again in their 30-4 season, they showed not just a will to win but also an ability to do it.

Their goal was not so high as a national championship, going into the season. Seniors Alford, Daryl Thomas and Todd Meier were quite aware that they could be the first four-year players in the Knight coaching era to leave IU without at least one Big Ten championship.

That didn't come until the last day of the season, and then with some help after their own season had ended. The scrambling continued right to the end at New Orleans three weeks later, each dodged bullet, each escape, each slipup a lesson learned and applied well.

The 74-73 final-game victory over Syracuse is an entry in history. Less known is that these national champions won three regular-season games by a point,

Bob Knight's pound on an
NCAA official table sent
a telephone bouncing and
ultimately cost him
and Indiana a $10,000 fine.

two more by two points, another – in the first year of the 3-point shot – by three points.

A loss in any of those games might have altered history. Because they were Big Ten champions and the highest-ranked midwestern team in the season-ending polls (No. 2 by UPI's coaches, No. 3 by AP's media voters), they got a No. 1 seed and assignment to the Hoosier Dome in Indianapolis. Maybe they would have won going elsewhere. It was a major plus for them that they got their tournament start in Hoosierland.

Maybe their biggest of those regular-season victories – by no means their best performance but maybe the most crucial – came in a game that did not figure to be either big or close.

Indiana went to Wisconsin as the No. 2-ranked team in the land, 11-1 in the Big Ten and 20-2 overall. Waiting was a Badger team that stood 1-11 in the Big Ten. The teams had met in Bloomington four weeks earlier. Indiana won that one 103-65, the margin established as early as 71-33 barely seven minutes into the second half.

There were warning signs of trouble at Madison.

Along with his 2,438 career points, Steve Alford included 385 assists, a few of them flashy.

Indiana's last previous game had been at Northwestern, against the team that shared the Big Ten basement with Wisconsin. Indiana had whipped Northwestern, 95-43, the biggest losing margin in Northwestern's basketball history. That happened the same weekend as the first Wisconsin game. In the rematch at Evanston, Indiana had barely won, 77-75. It wasn't quite that close; Northwestern bit into the margin with a 3-point basket just ahead of the buzzer.

Alford knew Wisconsin senior guard Mike Heineman well. Too well. Heineman and brother Chris were stars of the Connersville team that ended Alford's high school career one step short of the state tournament, then went on to win the championship. Heineman was 0-7 against Indiana and Alford as a collegian, and right from the beginning he was out to change that.

Heineman's first of three 3-point baskets started a 6-point Wisconsin run that opened a 22-12 early lead. He had 9 points in Wisconsin's 32-31 halftime lead.

Points were coming uncustomarily hard for Alford. He shot 4-for-13 at Northwestern, after successive games of 31, 42 and 30 – his IU high squeezed into the best

three-game run of his college career. That surge put him within 15 points of the IU career scoring record (2,192) that had belonged to Don Schlundt for 32 years.

Not then, but six years later, Alford admitted that as the record approached it was "a huge distraction…I was about to become No. 1 on a scoring list at a place where as a little kid I dreamed about playing."

He finally passed Schlundt with his second shot at Wisconsin, a 3-point basket. He was far from back in a groove. The deadliest 3-point shooter in IU history (.530 for his only season with the rule) closed the night at Wisconsin 2-for-11 on those, 4-for-19 overall, the highest number of misses – 3s or otherwise – in his IU career.

Three straight times, winding up regulation time and the first two overtimes, he shot for a game-winning basket but missed.

In the third overtime, Wisconsin led 85-84 when Alford rebounded a Badger free-throw miss, with 30 seconds left.

Heineman blanketed Alford as Joe Hillman brought the ball upcourt. When Alford couldn't shake free, Hillman took the ball into the deep left corner and shot an air ball, long. Dean Garrett fielded the ball like a pass and laid in the game winner at 0:04 – well past midnight back in Hoosier-engrossed Indiana.

In Alford's career, IU was 58-8 when he scored 20 points, 34-27 when he didn't. Northwestern and Wisconsin were two of the 34.

He averaged 21.6 the rest of the way as Indiana slipped twice on the road (at Purdue and Illinois the next-last weekend of the season), then beat Ohio State in the season finale. Later that afternoon, Michigan routed Purdue, so Indiana and Purdue shared the Big Ten title and Indiana got the No. 1 Mideast seed, with its Indianapolis routing.

A long, long night in Madison was a key to it all.

N A T I O N A L C H A M P I O N S

Indiana University

The very night that Indiana was outlasting Syracuse for the 1987 NCAA championship, Hollywood was giving out its Oscars. Up for two awards was *Hoosiers,* a masterpiece of basketball charm and hope. The film's fathers, writer and co-producer Angelo Pizzo and director David Anspaugh, are Hoosiers – Pizzo from Bloomington, Anspaugh from Decatur. They went to Indiana University together and entered film-making together. *Hoosiers* was their start.

But instead of attending the Oscar dinner, they watched the Indiana-Syracuse telecast at Anspaugh's house. "Once the game started – forget (the Oscars)," Pizzo said. "You go back to your roots in times of stress."

It was the perfect blending, *Hoosiers* and the 1986-87 Hoosiers. Never has a national championship run seemed more scripted, right down to The Shot – Keith Smart's, from left of the basket, distance about the same, as Jimmy Chitwood's climactic shot in *Hoosiers,* as Bobby Plump's decisive shot for Milan in the 1954 Indiana high school tournament final that *Hoosiers* fictionalized.

Daryl Thomas, Steve Alford and Dean Garrett celebrate on the awards stand at the Superdome.

The '87 Hoosiers were in trouble in their second tournament game, before a throaty band of 34,185 in the Hoosier Dome at Indianapolis. Auburn blew out to a 24-10 lead, fast.

Steve Alford, the one Indiana-raised starter for Knight's team, hadn't scored in those early minutes. He scored 10 points in less than two minutes when Indiana pulled within 38-37. He was 7-for-11 on 3-point shots in his 31-point game as Indiana roared away to a 107-90 victory.

(Top right) Even in New Orleans, the Indiana pep band made itself heard.

(Bottom right) Steve Alford's No. 12 showed up in some percussive places at the Superdome.

(Far right) Always and ever in Indiana lore: The Shot, by Keith Smart over Howard Triche to beat Syracuse, 74-73, in the last five seconds of the national championship game.

(Left) Keith Smart, twisting to score over Rony Seikaly, down the stretch 'made as many big plays in critical situations' as anybody Bob Knight has ever seen.

(Above right) Todd Meier, one of the 1987 champions' three seniors, gets some instructions from Bob Knight.

That, and their 92-58 opening victory over Fairfield, advanced them to Mideast Regional play at Riverfront Coliseum in Cincinnati.

Ricky Calloway was a Hoosier starter from Cincinnati. Indiana was in deep trouble in the Regional final against Louisiana State, down 75-66 with under five minutes to go when Calloway went up for a dunk, missed, and the ball rocketed off the rim out of bounds, with 4:38 to go.

Still the Hoosiers won. Joe Hillman came off the bench for just 53 seconds but converted Daryl Thomas's interception into a 3-point play that pulled Indiana within 75-71 – "a hell of a tough play, like a pinch-hit home run in the ninth inning," Knight said.

LSU led 76-75 when a one-and-one miss with 26 seconds to go gave Indiana the ball, and its victory chance. As the seconds ran down, Thomas went up for a 10-foot shot. He missed, but flying in was Calloway to catch the ball and, at 0:06, bank in the basket that won, 77-76.

That, and an earlier 88-82 victory over Duke in the first coaching matchup of Knight and his former Army captain, Mike Krzyzewski, sent the Hoosiers to the Final Four at the New Orleans Superdome.

Smart grew up in nearby Baton Rouge. As a Boy Scout, he had done some ushering in the Superdome. And now he was back.

Smart's role wasn't primary in the game that attracted all the pre-Final Four attention: No. 1-ranked Nevada-Las Vegas against Indiana, No. 2 in the final UPI coaches'

poll and No. 3 for AP's media; Knight's disciplined program against Jerry Tarkanian's operation that seemed always on propriety's edge.

The game's first surprise was that Indiana ran with free-wheeling UNLV. The second was that it ran very well.

Although Freddie Banks, in the first tournament with the 3-point shot, was firing up and hitting 3s at a rate not yet matched, although burly Armon Gilliam was ripping the Hoosiers inside, Indiana kept throwing in points. Indiana led 53-47 at halftime, but UNLV went ahead 59-57. Two Alford baskets launched an Indiana surge to a 73-65 lead that grew to 88-76 with 3:40 to play.

With 28 seconds left and Indiana's lead 92-88, Banks – 10-for-19 on 3s in a 38-point day – missed a one-and-one. Alford, a 90 percent lifetime shooter who in this game had, for the first time as a collegian, missed both halves of a two-shot chance, hit the one-and-one that widened the lead to 94-88.

When Banks missed again, Steve Eyl grabbed the rebound and broke out to the 3-point play that put the Hoosiers up 97-88 with 13 seconds left, enough time for UNLV only to slice the final margin to 97-93.

Gilliam (32) and Banks combined for 70 points, a two-man record against a Knight team. Guard Mark Wade set the NCAA tournament record that still stands with 18 assists. UNLV was 13-for-35 on 3s, Indiana just 2-for-4 – all by Alford, who scored 33 points.

Indiana-UNLV was the real national championship game, talk around New Orleans went. First-time finalist Syracuse's 77-63 victory over Big East rival Providence in the other semifinal game was unimpressive. Overlooked was No. 10-ranked Syracuse's 79-75 victory over No. 3 North Carolina to get to New Orleans.

Also ignored was how good the Orangemen were. Starters Derrick Coleman, Rony Seikaly and Sherman Douglas ultimately would be not only first-round NBA draft picks but also 10-year pros.

Alford hit two 3s closing out the first half for a 34-33 Indiana lead. A 15-3 Syracuse charge opened a 52-44 lead that was 52-46 with 12:12 to go when

(Top) Steve Alford's All-America career had a championship ending in New Orleans.

(Bottom) Keith Smart (23) and Dean Garrett (22) made Bob Knight happy he decided to look for help in junior colleges.

Smart re-entered the game.

Yes, he was there to hit the shot that won the national championship for the Hoosiers. Less remembered are all the other things he did in those last 12 minutes. He dropped a pass off to Thomas for a dunk. At 6-1, he drove the baseline and dived out at a 45-degree angle to hit a twisting shot over the 7-foot Seikaly. He drove to set up another Thomas basket, then freed himself with a quick move for a shot that tied the game, 61-61.

He made a backdoor cut and took a pass from Alford to score over the 6-10 Coleman. He tied the game at 70-70 with a baseline drive and reverse layup.

Then it was Syracuse ahead 73-70 and Howard Triche was shooting the second of two free throws for Syracuse, with 38 seconds left. Smart fielded the long rebound and drove straight upcourt to a 10-foot jump shot that put Indiana within 73-72. With 28 seconds left, Smart fouled Coleman. He missed, Thomas rebounded, and Indiana – as almost always, under Knight – ignored a time out and went straight to work, setting up a possible game-winner.

With Syracuse in a four-man zone and Douglas on him man-to-man, Alford faked a move to the left side of the court and broke sharply to the right. For an instant, Douglas was hung up and Alford was open "but it would have been a real tough pass," Alford said.

Instead, Smart took the ball to the left side, dropped a pass in to Thomas, took a return pass and drove at Thomas to get just enough of a screen on Triche to let him get away a 15-foot shot – The Shot. The only other NCAA championship game to swing from one team to the other on a late shot was North Carolina over Georgetown in 1982. That also was at the Superdome. That also was won by a shooter wearing No. 23, Michael Jordan.

The stunned Orangemen let three seconds tick away before getting a timeout at 0:01. Coleman's attempted floorlength pass was intercepted – by Smart. Dean Garrett, the other junior college transfer whose fit into the Hoosier lineup lifted a good team into a national champion, marveled later: "It was just all Keith, down the stretch."

Alford averaged 23 points a game and shot .618 on 3s in Indiana's six tournament games, with 23 points and a still-record seven 3s in the final game. But Smart (15.0 a game, 21 in the final game) was a deserving winner of the tournament's Outstanding Player Award. Smart, his Hoosier coach said that night, "made as many big plays in critical situations as anybody I've ever seen."

(Top) Sharan Alford, Steve's mother, shares a national-championship hug with Bob Knight.

(Bottom) Dean Garrett hugs Rick Calloway and Steve Eyl gazes as happy Hoosiers celebrate another championship.

Indiana 82   Purdue 79

Assembly Hall

January 30, 1988

D ean Garrett and Keith Smart were anomalies in the Indiana basketball program. Timely anomalies; they were vital to the Hoosiers' 1987 NCAA championship. Non-anomalies in the most important areas: dependable, hard-working, team-focused.

But they were junior college transfers, not the first nor the last of the Bob Knight era but – because of the '87 championship and Smart's title-winning shot – by far the most prominent.

(Left) A national symbol of courage, AIDS victim Ryan White, gets a hug, a gift and a courtside view of a victory from his favorite coach and team.

(Right) Dean Garrett gets a hero's rush from students after his game-winning basket against No. 2-ranked Purdue.

No.		Height	Class	G-S	Pts.
20	Ricky Calloway	6-6	Jr.	26-19	11.8
44	Joe Hillman	6-2	Jr.	27-16	7.1
22	Dean Garrett	6-10	Sr.	29-28	16.1
3	Jay Edwards	6-4	Fr.	23-15	15.6
23	Keith Smart	6-1	Sr.	29-21	13.2
32	Steve Eyl	6-6	Sr.	28-14	4.2
4	Lyndon Jones	6-1	Fr.	27-15	4.9
11	Todd Jadlow	6-9	Jr.	28-10	5.5
45	Brian Sloan	6-8	Jr.	19-3	2.2
14	Magnus Pelkowski	6-10	Jr.	20-3	3.1
42	Kreigh Smith	6-7	Jr.	18-0	2.4
35	Jeff Oliphant	6-5	So.	12-1	2.1

Garrett came in from California, Smart from Baton Rouge via his Garden City, Kan., Junior College. Their arrival as juniors meant they had skipped the usual two-year grounding in the Indiana game Knight juniors have. And it meant that they were fast-forwarded into the senior leadership his program has thrived on.

Each had benefited from that leadership, playing their first-year alongside what almost amounted to private tutors – senior tutors.

(Right) Some Bob Knight counsel for 1987 tournament hero Keith Smart.

(Bottom right) An Assembly Hall sendoff for the defending NCAA champions.

After Smart, just 3-for-8 on 3-point shots and averaging 9.6 per game in pre-conference play, opened his Big Ten career by going 5-for-5 on 3s and scoring 31 points at Ohio State, Alford pulled him aside for some of that senior counsel. Think ahead, not back, Alford told him. "If you have a good game, it's not your mom and dad who's going to see it in the paper, if you're playing at Michigan next it's (Antoine) Joubert and (Gary) Grant. Believe me, they're going to come at you. They don't want to see your name in the headlines anymore. They want to see theirs: 'Grant Stops Smart' or 'Joubert Stops Smart.'"

Garrett's counseling was daily. His arrival freed 6-7 Daryl Thomas to go back to his usual forward role, but the season Thomas spent at center gave him a working knowledge of how to play against every other veteran center in the league. Leading up to every game, even during games, he shared his "book" with Garrett. It was a relationship that got both deeply into each game.

When The Year After the Championship dawned, Smart and Garrett were the seniors, along with Steve Eyl. Leadership wasn't the only extra baggage they had added. They also were the reigning NCAA champion.

Indiana was 8-2 and No. 12-ranked nationally as Big Ten time came, the Hoosiers in the middle of five league teams in the Top 20 (Purdue and Michigan slightly ahead, Iowa and Illinois just below).

Then the trapdoor opened. For the first time since Knight's first year, the Hoosiers began 1-4 in the Big Ten – realistically all but eliminated from the championship race before January was over.

Obviously some changes were coming.

The most noted new additions to the Hoosier roster for 1987-88 were freshmen Jay Edwards and Lyndon Jones, who had led Marion to a feat unmatched in Indiana high school basketball in more than 60 years: three straight state championships. Edwards showed early he was an exceptional shooter. He started a December game. Then academic reports came in that Knight didn't like. He sat Edwards down in mid-December and kept him there through the first two Big Ten games, six games in all.

At Ohio State, that 1-4 league record as a backdrop, Knight for the first time started the two freshman guards.

The surgery was more radical than that. Knight restyled the Hoosier offense to include, in essence, three guards. This game, Smart wasn't one of them. Junior Joe Hillman – almost a prototypical Knight player at 6-2, 190, strong, tough, borderline-cocky and smart – was the third guard, the one whose defensive assignment would be a forward, normally 6-6 and up.

Benched with Smart was the other holdover starter from the national champions, junior Rick Calloway. Magnus Pelkowski, a 6-10 native of Bogota, Colombia, and Garrett were the big men in the Indiana lineup at Ohio State.

The result was stunning. Shooter Edwards had a tough night, 3-for-17, but his ballhandling teammate from high school days, Jones, blistered the Buckeyes with

At the Big Ten's other
Assembly Hall, Garrett plays
a glassy game with Ken Battle
(33) of the Flyin' Illini.

9-for-10 shooting and 21 points and Indiana won, 75-71.

All that was prelude to the arrival in town of the team that had emerged as the Big Ten's best: Purdue, 6-0 and out front in the league, 17-1 and No. 2-ranked nationally.

With no element of surprise left, with time for Purdue to capitalize in any way it could on the opportunities the small lineup provided, Knight opened the very same way against the Boilermakers.

And it was some opening. After 10 minutes, Indiana led 33-12.

Purdue was much too good for that early a knockout. The Boilermakers, down 52-37 at halftime, scored on their first six possessions of the second half to cut the gap to 58-50. They kept scoring and went around the Hoosiers, 71-69, but Edwards hit a 3. They led 74-72; Edwards hit another 3.

With 15 seconds to play, Purdue led 79-78 but Indiana took possession on a missed free throw. As Knight teams normally do, the Hoosiers disdained a timeout and went straight to work. "We didn't set it up," Garrett said, "but I knew the guys were looking for me."

Garrett came straight up from the baseline, took a pass from Jones and turned to put a jump shot just over defender Mel McCants' fingers. "It kinda rattled in,

but it dropped," said Garrett, who reached his career high in the game with 31 points.

Purdue got the clock stopped at 0:04 but turned the ball over in the backcourt and Jones scored at the buzzer for the 82-79 final margin.

The three-guard lineup took root. Jones (9 points and 7 assists) and Edwards (22 points and 5 assists) played all 40 minutes. Smart spelled Hillman (6 points, 5 assists, 5 rebounds) for two minutes. Calloway didn't play, and at the end of the year transferred to Kansas.

The Hoosiers went 10-3 closing out the Big Ten season. Edwards, the Big Ten Freshman of the Year, set a league record by going 8-for-9 on 3-point shots in scoring 36 points in a 91-85 victory at Minnesota. The Indiana springboard to the NCAA tournament was a 116-89 victory over Iowa, with Smart scoring a career-high 32.

The Hoosiers' NCAA reign ended quickly, though. Richmond stopped them in the first round at Hartford, Conn., 72-69.

1 9 8 7 – 1 9 8 8		
19-10; Big Ten 11-7, Fifth		
Miami, Ohio	W	90-65
Notre Dame	W	76-59
Kentucky [1]	*L	76-82
Vanderbilt	W	63-61
James Madison [2]	W	84-52
Washington State [2]	W	63-56
Eastern Kentucky	W	103-65
at Louisville	L	69-81
Pennsylvania [3]	W	94-54
Stanford [3]	W	83-73
at Iowa	L	70-84
at Northwestern	L	64-66
Wisconsin	W	55-53
at Michigan State	*L	74-75
Michigan	L	60-72
at Ohio State	W	75-71
Purdue	W	82-79
Minnesota	W	92-63
at Illinois	W	75-74
Northwestern	W	74-45
at Michigan	L	72-92
Michigan State	W	95-58
at Purdue	L	85-95
at Wisconsin	W	84-74
Illinois	L	65-75
Ohio State	W	85-77
at Minnesota	W	91-85
Iowa	W	116-89
N C A A		
Richmond [4]	L	69-72

* *Overtime*
[1] *Big Four Classic, Hoosier Dome*
[2] *Indiana Classic*
[3] *Hoosier Classic, Indianapolis*
[4] *at Hartford, Connecticut*

Indiana 76 Michigan 75

Assembly Hall

February 19, 1989

The 1988-89 Bob Knight sweater had a tendency to inch up, but official Eric Harmon doesn't notice.

When the year began, Michigan and Illinois were considered national threats. Each had lots back from strong clubs. And the rankings were right. The Wolverines and Illini wound up playing against each other in a Final Four classic, which Michigan won and went on to take its only NCAA championship in overtime against Seton Hall.

But the Big Ten champion was Indiana, thanks in large part to two one-point victories over those national-champion Wolverines.

This was a Hoosier team that benefited richly from its experiences of the year before. One more time, when things looked bleak, Indiana coach Bob Knight spurned convention and went to a three-guard lineup – the same three guards: Joe Hillman, now a senior, and Lyndon Jones and Jay Edwards, now sophomores.

Not just Michigan and Illinois but also Iowa all were in the Top 10 when the season opened. Knight questioned the advisability of playing such teams without three rebounders, without three big defenders. Not until his team had been pummeled for more than 100 points three times – 102-78 by Syracuse, 106-92 by North Carolina, 101-79 by Louisville, all in a 12-day stretch, three of just the six times Indiana opponents reached 100 in Knight's first 25 years – did Knight decide his best lineup used those three guards.

No.		Height	Class	G-S	Pts.
32	Eric Anderson	6-9	Fr.	34-32	11.9
44	Joe Hillman	6-2	Sr.	34-34	12.6
11	Todd Jadlow	6-9	Sr.	34-28	10.6
3	Jay Edwards*	6-4	So.	34-33	20.0
4	Lyndon Jones	6-1	So.	34-29	8.4
5	Chuckie White	6-7	Jr.	32-5	4.4
10	Mark Robinson	6-5	Jr.	29-4	3.7
23	Jamal Meeks	6-0	Fr.	35-1	2.8
45	Brian Sloan	6-8	Sr.	34-7	2.7
14	Magnus Pelkowski	6-10	Sr.	17-1	2.4
42	Kreigh Smith	6-7	Sr.	15-1	3.3
35	Jeff Oliphant	6-5	Jr.	21-0	1.9
21	Mike D'Aloisio	6-4	Sr.	18-0	1.1

* All-Big Ten

(Left) For Dr. Brad Bomba, Bob Knight and assistant coach Ron Felling, things always are looking up on the sidelines at Minnesota's Williams Arena.

(Right) Brian Sloan's elevator is going up as fake-launched defenders come down.

(Left) Eric Anderson, Freshman of the Year for the league champions.

(Right) Jay Edwards, driving here, a few minutes later just did beat the clock and future national-champion Michigan.

Todd Jadlow scored 32 points without a miss against Iowa, but it's Bob Knight making points here.

It didn't immediately pay off in victory. The Hoosiers lost at Notre Dame, 84-71. Then things clicked — seven wins in a row going into Big Ten play, then a 6-0 start in league play that included surprises at Purdue (74-73) and at Michigan (71-70). The Purdue win got Knight past one-time Purdue coach "Piggy" Lambert for the Big Ten career record, and a victory over Northwestern was the 48-year-old Knight's 500th.

The 13-game winning streak ended in a 75-65 loss at Illinois, but the Hoosiers came right back with a gem: 104-89 over No. 9-ranked Iowa, center Todd Jadlow scoring 32 points by going 7-for-7 from the field and 18-for-18 on free throws — before missing his last shot and two free throws. The Hoosiers stood 10-1 when Michigan (7-4) came into The Hall for a Sunday afternoon national TV game. The Sunday before, the nation had watched Purdue fight the Hoosiers to the finish

only to lose to Edwards' tie-breaking jump shot with four seconds to go, 64-62.

Michigan countered the three-guard approach with four big, athletic starters, 6-7 and up. This time, the Wolverines had an unexpected problem: star Glen Rice couldn't score. How much of the reason was defender Hillman, five inches shorter, who could know? Hillman's role in this championship season ever since has put him with Quinn Buckner on a very short Knight list of extraordinary leaders. And his matchup this day? Rice was to win the Outstanding Player Award in the NCAA finals. Rice was to set a Big Ten career scoring record and make first-team All-America. Rice was to lead the Big Ten in scoring (for a second straight year) with a 24.8 average, and he was to go on to the NBA and become an all-star.

This day, he scored the game's first basket, then made only one other shot all day and finished with 7 points.

But guard Rumeal Robinson, who was to hit the free throws that made Michigan the national champion over Seton Hall, picked up for Rice with 24 points and the battle raged.

The Wolverines led 72-71 when Sean Higgins sank a 3 — the lead now 75-71 with just 1:08 left. Two free throws by Edwards at 0:54 cut the lead to 75-73, and Michigan patiently ran the 45-second shot clock down. Just before it ran out, the Wolverines missed, Indiana rebounded, and Jones rushed the ball upcourt, looking for Edwards.

Indiana's rise from December humiliation to the championship in the nation's strongest conference made Bob Knight the consensus national Coach of the Year.

Hoosiers Brian Sloan (45), Eric Anderson (32), Lyndon Jones (4) and Joe Hillman join the bench in celebrating a 71-70 victory at Michigan.

Barely in time, he almost handed the ball off, and in one fast, fluid motion, a good three feet into 3-point range, Edwards went up, and shot, and hit.

Long before the ball hit net, the buzzer sounded. Michigan coach Bill Frieder argued the shot was late and commandeered a TV monitor. It was breathtakingly close even with stop-action but it appeared that the ball left Edwards' fingers just before the last 10th of a second ticked off. "I'm not going to comment," Frieder said after his look. "I'll get ripped if I say it was good because people will say I'm not standing up for my team and I'll get ripped if I say it wasn't good because they'll say I was making excuses."

It was Edwards' only 3 in a 23-point performance.

The Hoosiers won two more and then clinched at least a share of the championship by winning at Ohio State, 73-66. That night, Edwards had 20 points in the first 11 minutes and he missed a 3-point shot that would have given him 30 at halftime. He finished with 34.

The clear-cut title-clincher came a game later over Wisconsin, and then Knight chose, for various reasons, to rest his key players – Edwards (sore back), Jadlow (bruised thigh), Hillman and Big Ten Freshman of the Year Eric Anderson – in a meaningless 87-70 season-closer at Iowa. Maybe he was punished for that. Seeds came out the next day and Illinois, ostensibly off its two victories over Indiana, was given the No. 1 Mideast seed and assigned to Indianapolis while Indiana was made the No. 2 seed in the West Regional. At Tucson,

the Hoosiers routed George Mason and Texas-El Paso, but Seton Hall closed the 27-8 season for Indiana with a 78-65 victory at Denver and moved on to join Illinois and Michigan at Seattle.

Already by then, Jay Edwards – a second-team All-America pick and media choice as Big Ten Player of the Year, though the silver basketball as league MVP went to Michigan's Rice – had announced his two-year college career was over. He declared for the NBA draft.

Knight, for the recovery from the awful start and the run to a championship in a big Big Ten year, was the national Coach of the Year.

Two years later, one of his November conquerors, Jim Boeheim of Syracuse, affirmed that coaching award.

"That year, that coaching, that team winning the Big Ten is the biggest upset of all my time in basketball," Boeheim said when both Indiana and Syracuse were in Hawaii for a 1990-91 tournament.

"That team had no business winning it. There's no way conceivably with the talent in that league that year that that team could have won that league.

"That was just a great, great coaching job."

1988 – 1989		
27-8; Big Ten 15-3, Champion		
Illinois State [1]	W	83-48
Stanford [1]	W	84-73
Syracuse [2]	L	78-102
North Carolina [2]	L	92-106
at Miami, Ohio	W	87-70
Louisville [3]	L	79-101
at Notre Dame	L	71-84
Virginia Commonwealth [4]	W	85-68
Santa Clara [4]	W	64-49
Arkansas-L.R.	W	105-77
Texas-El Paso	W	81-63
at Kentucky	W	75-52
St. Bonaventure [5]	W	103-66
Utah State [5]	W	73-61
Ohio State	W	75-65
at Purdue	W	74-73
Northwestern	W	92-76
at Wisconsin	*W	61-58
Michigan State	W	75-60
at Michigan	W	71-70
at Illinois	L	65-75
Iowa	W	104-89
Minnesota	W	66-62
at Northwestern	W	72-56
Purdue	W	64-62
Michigan	W	76-75
at Michigan State	W	76-65
at Minnesota	W	75-62
at Ohio State	W	73-66
Illinois	L	67-70
Wisconsin	W	75-64
at Iowa	L	70-87
N C A A		
George Mason [6]	W	99-85
Texas-El Paso [6]	W	92-69
Seton Hall [7]	L	65-78

* Overtime
[1] Pre-Season NIT, Assembly Hall
[2] Pre-Season NIT, New York
[3] Big Four Classic, Hoosier Dome
[4] Indiana Classic
[5] Hoosier Classic, Indianapolis
[6] at Tucson, Arizona
[7] at Denver, Colorado

Indiana 69 Michigan 67

Assembly Hall

January 8, 1990

Bob Knight's Senior Day talk in Year of Freshmen.

Since going to the Final Four with freshman guards Quinn Buckner and Jim Crews in the first year under the modern freshman-eligibility rule, Bob Knight never has been reluctant to give rookies a chance to play.

All standards for Knight use of freshmen probably always will come from the 1989-90 season when:

Of the 145 starting assignments, 73 went to true freshmen, straight out of high school; and of the 90 starting

roles in the 18 Big Ten games, 45 went to true freshmen.

Add in red-shirt freshman Matt Nover and those figures become 87 starts overall, 54 in Big Ten play – or exactly three freshmen per game in each category.

The rookies, Nover included, responded by scoring 65 percent of the team's points and contributing 55 percent of its rebounds, and 57 percent of its assists. Also, 61 percent of its turnovers – in an 18-11 season, 8-10 in Big Ten play. Obviously, there was a price for learning on the job.

As early as the second game of the year, Knight started three freshmen and two sophomores. The Hoosiers won Game 4 from Notre Dame with four freshman starters and sophomore Eric Anderson – who, like Nover, actually had graduated from high school a bit early, neither of them 18 on diploma day.

Against Notre Dame, they may have been the youngest lineup ever to open a game for a nationally ranked team. The starters for the 14th-ranked Hoosiers

No.		Height	Class	G-S	Pts.
40	Calbert Cheaney	6-6	Fr.	29-29	17.1
32	Eric Anderson	6-9	So.	29-28	16.3
24	Matt Nover	6-8	Fr.	26-14	5.3
23	Jamal Meeks	6-0	So.	28-13	4.0
20	Greg Graham	6-4	Fr.	29-16	9.7
4	Lyndon Jones	6-1	Jr.	22-12	6.1
33	Pat Graham	6-5	Fr.	29-4	7.7
21	Chris Reynolds	6-1	Fr.	28-12	3.2
54	Chris Lawson	6-9	Fr.	27-7	3.6
30	Todd Leary	6-2	Fr.	22-2	2.3
10	Mark Robinson	6-5	Sr.	21-5	3.2
35	Jeff Oliphant	6-5	Sr.	13-0	2.5
34	Lawrence Funderburke	6-8	Fr.	6-3	11.7

(Top) Almost pleading, Bob Knight works to communicate with his youngest team.

(Bottom left) Rookie Greg Graham shoots a high-percentage shot.

(Bottom right) Lyndon Jones, a junior leader with a special background, takes the ball to the basket.

that night averaged 18.82 years old. The starting combination at Iowa a month later maybe have been the youngest up to then ever to start and win a Big Ten game (18.88). Even two years later when Michigan had its "Fab Five" freshmen, the average age when that group made its first start (also against Notre Dame) was 18.84; the average for its first winning Big Ten start (also against Iowa) 18.85.

The two Indiana combinations were not the same. Ohioan Lawrence Funderburke had been the other freshman starter, with Calbert Cheaney, in the season opener. The Notre Dame game was Funderburke's third and last Indiana start; 10 days later, after semester exams, he left the team and ultimately finished his career at

Rookie Calbert Cheaney (40), making his mark early, claims a rebound over Eric Anderson.

Ohio State. Nover, Cheaney, Greg Graham and Chris Reynolds were the freshman starters at Iowa, along with sophomore Anderson.

Funderburke's departure injected some controversy into the young Hoosier team's December, but for the most part it went dreamily. Cheaney was the best of the freshmen from the first day of practice, and he was 9-for-11 in scoring 20 points in the opening win over Miami of Ohio. Greg Graham scored 24 points in a second-game victory over Kent State. Pat Graham came off the bench to hit three straight 3s in a 71-69 scrape past Kentucky before 40,128 at the Hoosier Dome. Reynolds got his first college start in the Notre Dame game and had 14 points, 7 assists and 5 steals.

The day after Funderburke left, the Hoosiers found themselves in major trouble at Texas-El Paso, where freshman Steve Alford had a long day six years earlier. This time, Indiana led 61-52 with 6½ minutes left, but future Indiana Pacer Antonio Davis (15 points, 8 rebounds) led a comeback that gave TV-watching Hoosiers their first look at Cheaney under pressure.

The rookie from Evansville Harrison, Knight's first left-handed starter in 19 Indiana seasons, drove the baseline for a reverse layup that widened the lead. UTEP caught up at 63-63, but Cheaney broke the tie with a one-and-one conversion at 2:38, then drove the baseline one more time for the basket at 1:19 that opened 69-64 daylight in an eventual 69-66 victory.

The Hoosiers went into the New Year 10-0. Ever-apprehensive, Knight feared success had come too quickly and too easily for the young club. Now, it was No. 9 in the polls and shooting .543, with Cheaney, Anderson, Nover and Pat Graham each well over .600.

In 1983, a senior-filled Indiana team had gone 10-0 and opened with a 70-67 loss at Ohio State. This team also opened its league season at Ohio State, against a 5-4

Buckeye team with its own touted freshman, Jimmy Jackson. Jackson, in the first of many superb square-offs the two were to have over the next three years, outscored Cheaney, 19-18, and Ohio State won the game, 69-67.

The rookies' balloon was popped. They were 0-1 in the conference, going home to take on the reigning national champion, No. 3-ranked Michigan, 10-1 with Rumeal Robinson, Terry Mills, Loy Vaught, Sean Higgins – virtually everyone but Glen Rice – back from the title run.

Very early, it was a mismatch. Michigan put the reeling Hoosiers down 13-6, then 27-12. Cheaney stopped an eight-point Michigan run with a free throw, but three quick Wolverine baskets opened an embarrassing 33-13 gap with 9½ first-half minutes still to go.

Somehow, some way, the youngest Indiana team ever put together the biggest Hoosier comeback in Assembly Hall history.

Michigan's lead still was 40-26 at halftime, 64-52 with just under eight minutes to go. There, it was veteran Michigan, not Indiana, that Wolverines coach Steve Fisher said "lost our poise, and composure, and the game – maybe in that order."

The Hoosier thunderbolt was a 7-0 burst in 43 seconds. Greg Graham scored, then missed a free throw but Cheaney rebounded for a basket. After a Michigan miss, Lyndon Jones hit a 3. With 6:30 still to go, the game that had seemed over was a 64-61 scramble and 17,243 made Assembly Hall deafening. With 2:21 left, Cheaney rebounded another Indiana miss and hit a one-and-one that gave Indiana a 65-64 lead. With 40 seconds to go, the run had grown to 17-0, Indiana led 69-64, and the loud crowd was victory-bound. The game ended 69-67.

The radical swings of the Michigan game proved typical of the Hoosier season. Playing its third game

in six nights, Indiana opened a 16-point lead on Purdue in the first half and then lost in overtime, 81-79, despite a career-high 30 points by Anderson. With five freshmen on the court for more than 10 stretch minutes, the Hoosiers won a big game at Iowa, 83-79, then came home and took the second-worst beating an Indiana team ever had at Assembly Hall, 75-57 against Michigan State (the worst: 79-60 by Minnesota in 1976-77, a game ultimately awarded to Indiana by forfeit).

The Hoosiers became the first Big Ten team to make the NCAA tournament field with a losing league record. They didn't stay long; California ended their season with a 65-63 victory at the same place the 1987-88 season had ended with a first-round tournament loss, Hartford, Conn.

1 9 8 9 – 1 9 9 0		
18-11; Big Ten, 8-10, Seventh		
Miami, Ohio	W	77-66
Kent State	W	79-68
Kentucky [1]	W	71-69
Notre Dame	W	81-72
South Alabama [2]	W	96-67
Long Beach State [2]	W	92-75
at Texas-El Paso	W	69-66
Iowa State	W	115-66
Wichita State [3]	W	75-54
Texas A&M [3]	W	94-66
at Ohio State	L	67-69
Michigan	W	69-67
at Northwestern	W	77-63
Purdue	*L	79-81
at Iowa	W	83-79
Michigan State	L	57-75
at Minnesota	L	89-108
Wisconsin	W	85-61
at Illinois	L	65-70
at Michigan	L	71-79
Northwestern	W	98-75
Iowa	W	118-71
at Purdue	L	49-72
at Michigan State	L	66-72
Minnesota	L	70-75
at Wisconsin	W	70-68
Ohio State	W	77-66
Illinois	L	63-69
N C A A		
California [4]	L	63-65

* Overtime
[1] *Big Four Classic, Hoosier Dome*
[2] *Indiana Classic*
[3] *Hoosier Classic, Indianapolis*
[4] *at Hartford, Connecticut*

117

Indiana 82   Florida State 60
Freedom Hall   Louisville, Kentucky

March 16, 1991

Mid-season election to the Basketball Hall of Fame came for Bob Knight at 50, but that's not his topic in a one-sided chat with assistant Ron Felling.

It was a year in which Indiana closed the gap on basketball greatness – never quite arrived there but got enough glimpses of it to know it was within reach.

For a long, long time on a Sunday afternoon at Ohio State's St. John Arena in what may have been the best college game of the year, the Hoosiers seemed to have made it to the top level. But they slipped.

They still talk about that Feb. 17 game in Columbus, as is the winners' wont. No. 2-ranked Ohio State topped No. 4 Indiana, 97-95, in double overtime. Calbert Cheaney (26 points) and freshman Damon Bailey (32) led balanced Indiana against Ohio State and Jimmy Jackson, who had 30 points and lots of help. The game-turning play came with 22 seconds left in regulation time, Indiana up 77-74 with the ball in Cheaney's hands and the shot clock running down. From near center court, Cheaney started to drive but 6-8 Treg Lee came off his own man to poke the ball away and grab it. In an involuntary lunge to reclaim the ball, Cheaney drew his fifth foul. Just before the buzzer, Jackson drove to a tying layup and, with five seconds left in the second

overtime, Lee broke the game's 20th tie with a short baseline jump shot.

Ohio State had turned back a late Indiana surge to win at Assembly Hall in the teams' first meeting, 93-85, a game with its own bit of uniqueness. In the entire competitive history of young Bailey – who started playing for school teams as a fourth-grader at Heltonville Elementary and went on to Shawswick Junior High,

No.		Height	Class	G-S	Pts.
40	Calbert Cheaney*	6-6	So.	34-34	21.6
32	Eric Anderson*	6-9	Jr.	34-34	13.7
24	Matt Nover	6-8	So.	34-26	6.9
22	Damon Bailey	6-3	Fr.	33-14	11.4
23	Jamal Meeks	6-0	Jr.	34-26	3.5
20	Greg Graham	6-4	So.	34-13	8.7
4	Lyndon Jones	6-1	Sr.	34-10	3.9
33	Pat Graham	6-5	So.	34-4	7.4
21	Chris Reynolds	6-1	So.	33-4	4.1
54	Chris Lawson	6-9	So.	27-5	3.6
25	Pat Knight	6-6	Fr.	22-0	1.8

* All-Big Ten

Sophomore Calbert Cheaney made big strides toward his future All-America and College Player of the Year status, but one of his best performances of the season ended in dismay at Ohio State.

Undersized center Matt Nover heads for the basket against Ohio State's Treg Lee.

Bedford North Lawrence High and IU – it was the first time his team ever lost a home game.

Ironically, four nights after the double-overtime loss at Ohio State, the Hoosiers lost again at Assembly Hall, to Iowa 80-79 in overtime on a tip-in at the buzzer, and Bailey that time for the first time in his basketball life was shut out – in what was to be the last home-court loss of his IU years: two home losses in a scholastic career covering 13 years.

The back-to-back losses after a 22-2 start sank the Hoosiers 2½ games back of Ohio State with five games to go (four for the Buckeyes). The league race seemed decided, but Indiana won its last five and Ohio State lost at Purdue, then on the final day at Iowa, and the two teams were co-champions at 15-3.

Indiana went into the NCAA tournament No. 3-ranked in the land, though NCAA selectors skipped over that to give No. 5 Ohio State a top seed and make Indiana the second seed in a regional field topped by No. 2-ranked Arkansas.

The Hoosiers had saved their showiest basketball of the season for the tournament, and for thousands of their southern Indiana fans who had to go only across the river to Louisville's Freedom Hall to back them in Rounds 1 and 2.

After a 79-69 first-rounder with Coastal Carolina, Indiana fell behind Florida State, 36-25. A Seminole guard named Charlie Ward – two years from becoming football's Heisman Trophy winner – was bedeviling the Hoosiers with five early steals. Bailey hit a 3 at 0:05 so the halftime deficit was just 38-32.

Indiana won, 82-60. That's a 50-22 difference in a second-half performance to put alongside the 57-33 jewel against Michigan that capped the 1976 championship season. This one was 57-24 from the 36-25 nadir.

Awaiting a chance to return are (from left) Calbert Cheaney, Damon Bailey, Jamal Meeks, Matt Nover and Eric Anderson.

Opening the second half, Cheaney hit a 3, the Hoosiers got the ball back, and Pat Graham hit a 3. Florida State led 40-39 when Pat Graham hit another 3, then Cheaney another. The loud crowd response "got their players energized," Kennedy said. "You could see it in their eyes, once they started drilling the 3-point shots. They just took off."

Even Knight was surprised with some of the second-half numbers. The Hoosiers didn't commit a turnover in the last 23 minutes, and they shot .643 for the second half. In one stretch spanning halftime, they hit six straight 3s. From the 38-29 low point, the Hoosiers outscored their dazed opponents, 36-9.

"I would like to have heard Coach Knight's halftime talk," Kennedy said. "They just played so hard, and so well."

They moved on to Charlotte and experienced the other end of the 3-point gunbarrel. Kansas hit six 3s in the first six minutes to explode out front 13-2 and 23-4. About then, a board came loose in midcourt and officials told both coaches play had to stop. "Fine," Knight said. "Why don't we start over tomorrow?" It was the best answer he had available for that dilemma and the Jayhawks won 83-65, on their way to a Final Four runnerup finish to Duke at the Hoosier Dome.

Jamal Meeks finds just a bit of daylight against Ohio State's Perry Carter and Jimmy Jackson.

1 9 9 0 – 1 9 9 1		
29-5; Big Ten 15-3, Co-champion		
Northeastern [1]	W	100-78
Santa Clara [1]	W	73-69
Syracuse [1]	L	74-77
at Notre Dame	W	70-67
Louisville [2]	W	72-52
at Vanderbilt	W	84-73
Niagara [3]	W	101-64
San Diego [3]	W	91-64
Western Michigan	W	97-68
Kentucky	W	87-84
at Iowa State	W	87-76
Marshall [4]	W	91-67
Ohio [4]	W	102-64
Illinois	W	109-74
Northwestern	W	99-58
at Purdue	W	65-62
at Iowa	W	99-79
Ohio State	L	85-93
at Michigan	W	70-60
Michigan State	W	97-63
Wisconsin	W	73-57
at Minnesota	W	77-66
at Northwestern	W	105-74
Purdue	W	81-63
at Ohio State	**L	95-97
Iowa	*L	79-80
Michigan	W	112-79
at Michigan State	W	62-56
at Wisconsin	W	74-61
Minnesota	W	75-59
at Illinois	W	70-58
N C A A		
Coastal Carolina [5]	W	79-69
Florida State [5]	W	82-60
Kansas [6]	L	65-83

* *Overtime*
** *Double Overtime*
[1] *Maui Classic*
[2] *Big Four Classic, Hoosier Dome*
[3] *Indiana Classic*
[4] *Hoosier Classic, Indianapolis*
[5] *at Louisville, Kentucky*
[6] *at Charlotte, North Carolina*

Indiana 86 Ohio State 80
St. John Arena Columbus, Ohio
February 23, 1992

E arly in the Bob Knight years, Indiana became the wild-card rivalry for the entire Big Ten. When Northwestern and Wisconsin had trouble filling their arenas for other games, the annual Indiana visit packed their houses. It was always true at Purdue, but when at varying times Minnesota, Michigan, Ohio State, Michigan State, Iowa and Illinois became national powers, Indiana was the choice target – Indiana and Knight, Indiana because of Knight.

Over those first 25 Knight years, the peak in sustained team-against-team basketball performance – two-way,

Victory nets a smile, and a Final Four trip, for Bob Knight at Albuquerque.

No.		Height	Class	G-S	Pts.
40	Calbert Cheaney*	6-6	Jr.	34-32	17.6
44	Alan Henderson	6-9	Fr.	33-26	11.6
32	Eric Anderson	6-9	Sr.	34-24	10.9
22	Damon Bailey	6-3	So.	34-27	12.4
21	Chris Reynolds	6-1	Jr.	33-24	4.3
20	Greg Graham	6-4	Jr.	34-16	12.8
23	Jamal Meeks	6-0	Sr.	32-4	3.6
24	Matt Nover	6-8	Jr.	34-16	6.5
50	Todd Lindeman	7-0	Fr.	20-0	3.2
30	Todd Leary	6-3	So.	22-1	3.8

All-Big Ten

all-out, great players playing brilliantly – may have come in the four games Indiana and Ohio State played in the 1991 and '92 Big Ten seasons. And the two teams weren't far from having a fifth, final matchup for the 1992 NCAA championship in the Minneapolis Metrodome. It would have been perfect, the final, tie-breaking settlement. The nation deserved to be cut in on the fun.

In retrospect, the two teams' games over those two years may have been *too* big, *too* good, *too* prized – particularly the second and theoretically decisive game each year. There is evidence that each team had trouble reaching so high a peak again, at least for a while.

Calbert Cheaney and Jimmy Jackson were the lead warriors. Jackson, out of Toledo, was the top-rated high

(Left) Eric Anderson puts up a stop sign against Duke's Christian Laettner on a rare 8-point Laettner day.

(Right) Calbert Cheaney achieves re-entry after a Final Four dunk.

Calbert Cheaney's record career point total included a few easy ones.

school player in the country when he picked Ohio State. Cheaney, out of Evansville, might have played his way into elite ranking or, far more important to him, into the state championship role that Jackson enjoyed, but for a foot fracture that short-circuited his senior season.

They met in the first Big Ten game either ever played. Indiana was 10-0 and freshman Cheaney was the primary reason, but freshman Jackson was the key to Ohio State's 69-67 victory at Columbus. Indiana got even, 77-66, at Assembly Hall. Jackson's point edge was 19-18 at Columbus, Cheaney's 22-12 in Bloomington.

Those were low-key compared to their sophomore meetings. Jackson scored 20 points when unbeaten, No. 4-ranked Ohio State opened a 22-point lead at Assembly Hall, saw it shrink to 3, then held off No. 3 Indiana to win, 93-85, despite 28 Cheaney points. In their rematch at St. John Arena, Jackson had 30 and Cheaney 26 in the No. 2 Buckeyes' 97-95 double-overtime victory over No. 4 Indiana. They met again in

January '92 at Assembly Hall in a game that reversed the '91 game there. This time, Indiana went up by 19 points in the second half, Ohio State unloaded a 26-2 wallop that put the Bucks up 63-59 with seven minutes left, and Indiana counter-rallied for a 91-83 victory. Jackson had 30 points that night; Cheaney, limited to 25 minutes by foul trouble, had 16.

There were, of course, lots of other telling games for both teams in 1991-92 and they handled them well enough that each hung in the Top 10 nationally. Indiana, in particular, had some miraculous performances. The Cincinnati team that was to reach the Final Four took an 81-60 beating on its home court in December. Ten times Indiana won by 30 or more points, including – just before going to Columbus – 103-73 over the Michigan State team that had ended a 6-0 Hoosier jumpout in the Big Ten with a 76-60 victory at East Lansing.

The Big Ten race had settled down to them – Indiana 10-2 (and 19-4 overall, No. 7 in the land) and Ohio State 9-2 (17-4 overall, No. 6 in the polls) – when they met the second time. The circumstances duplicated the classic double-overtime of the year before: a February Sunday afternoon in St. John Arena, on national TV.

This was where Damon Bailey had scored 32 points as a rookie. This time, Bailey missed everything with an early 3-point try and the packed house dogged him with chants of "Air ball!" every subsequent handling – till the last minute before halftime when he broke a 36-36 tie with a 3, then beat the buzzer with another to send Indiana in at the break with a 42-38 lead.

When the teams had met at Bloomington, Indiana's

Alan Henderson was out with flu. Henderson packed both games into this one and nailed the Buckeyes for 24 points.

Cheaney had never shaken memories of that double-overtime loss, of the 77-74 lead the Hoosiers held with the ball in his hands and less than 30 seconds to play. He lost the ball on a dribble, committed his fifth foul, and watched through those remarkable, excruciating overtimes as victory swung to Ohio State.

"We were in a position to *win* that game," Cheaney said one more time after this game. "That play has hung in my mind since I made it."

This time, after Ohio State had scored six straight points to tie the game at 62, Cheaney broke the tie with a basket, then rebounded a Buckeye miss and hurried downcourt to sink a 3.

The wedge had been established. Indiana jumped that lead on up to 75-64 and won, 86-80.

"We finally went in there and won," Cheaney said. "I don't think (the play that he said had hung in his mind) will hang there much anymore."

This was to be the last Cheaney-Jackson meeting as collegians, Jackson giving up his senior year to turn pro. This time, Cheaney had 28, Jackson 24, and over their joint careers their teams had broken even.

The year before, Ohio State after its Indiana sweep had seemed home free as league champion, especially after Indiana followed the double-overtime loss with an overtime defeat at home against Iowa. But the Buckeyes lost two of their last three games and Indiana salvaged a co-championship.

This time, Indiana – promoted to No. 2 in the land after the second win over the Buckeyes – lost two of its last three games (at Michigan and Purdue) to hand a clear-cut championship to Ohio State.

It was the first time in 11 Big Ten stretch runs that Indiana had faltered and lost. The Hoosiers found the only soothing answer: a tournament run that swept them past LSU (and Shaquille O'Neal), Florida State and UCLA for a trip to the Final Four.

Ohio State never made the Final Four in the Jackson era. The Buckeyes just missed, losing in the regional final in overtime – to Michigan, and its freshmen. Indiana's run ended in the national semifinals, 81-78 to Duke. Duke blew Michigan away in the championship game, the one that – with just a change or two – could have been Ohio State-Indiana V.

At a post-season team autograph session, Damon Bailey's table had a long line.

1 9 9 1 – 1 9 9 2		
27-7; Big Ten 14-4, Second		
UCLA [1]	L	72-87
Butler	W	97-73
Notre Dame	W	78-46
Kentucky [2]	L	74-76
Vanderbilt	W	88-51
Boston University [3]	W	88-47
Central Michigan [3]	W	99-52
St. John's [4]	W	82-77
Texas Tech [5]	W	86-69
Indiana State [5]	W	94-44
at Cincinnati	W	81-60
Minnesota	W	96-50
at Wisconsin	W	79-63
Ohio State	W	91-83
at Northwestern	W	96-62
Michigan	W	89-74
Purdue	W	106-65
at Michigan State	L	60-76
at Illinois	W	76-65
Iowa	W	81-66
at Minnesota	L	67-71
Northwestern	W	91-60
Michigan State	W	103-73
at Ohio State	W	86-80
Illinois	W	76-70
at Iowa	W	64-60
at Michigan	L	60-68
Wisconsin	W	66-41
at Purdue	L	59-61
N C A A		
Eastern Illinois [6]	W	94-55
LSU [6]	W	89-79
Florida State [7]	W	85-74
UCLA [7]	W	106-79
Duke [8]	L	78-81

[1] *Tipoff Classic, Springfield, Mass.*
[2] *Hoosier Dome, Indianapolis*
[3] *Indiana Classic*
[4] *100th Anniversary Game, Madison Square Garden, NY*
[5] *Hoosier Classic, Indianapolis*
[6] *at Boise, Idaho*
[7] *at Albuquerque, New Mexico*
[8] *at Minneapolis, Minnesota*

Indiana 86 Minnesota 75

Williams Arena Minneapolis, Minnesota

February 27, 1993

College Player of Year Calbert Cheaney gets a quick message from Bob Knight.

126

I t was a Friday afternoon, too early for spring, but Bloomington was in bloom. Electric. Excited. Expectant. Indiana was No. 1 in the country, 12-0 and moving out in the Big Ten. And Purdue was coming to town on Sunday. A brisk practice this afternoon, a walk-through and some touching up on Saturday, then Glenn Robinson and the Boilermakers, in Assembly Hall. And in four more weeks, the start of the NCAA tournament.

And then it happened.

A quick turnover in scrimmaging between the starters and reserves. A lead pass to Alan Henderson, behind everybody. A leap to field the pass, a clean catch, a slightly awkward landing, for just an instant all of Henderson's weight on his right knee. It buckled.

The leading rebounder on the leading team in the country lay sprawled on the court, in agony, his season for all practical purposes over.

Pat Graham, his own career hampered by a string of injuries, that very weekend was coming back from nearly three months of recovery from a foot injury. Graham was in the scrimmage, maybe 20 feet away when Henderson went down. "I saw his knee buckle," Graham said. "I thought I was going to get sick." Chris Reynolds said, "I just went numb inside."

Tests that night and the next day confirmed the worst: torn anterior cruciate ligament.

Caesar was warned about the ides of March. Knight might be wondering about the middle of February.

No.		Height	Class	G-S	Pts.
40	Calbert Cheaney*	6-6	Sr.	35-35	22.4
44	Alan Henderson	6-9	So.	30-25	11.1
24	Matt Nover	6-8	Sr.	35-35	11.0
20	Greg Graham*	6-4	Sr.	35-32	16.5
22	Damon Bailey	6-3	Jr.	35-24	10.1
21	Chris Reynolds	6-1	Sr.	35-13	3.2
33	Pat Graham	6-5	Jr.	13-3	6.5
34	Brian Evans	6-8	Fr.	35-4	5.3
30	Todd Leary	6-3	Jr.	35-4	4.8
25	Pat Knight	6-6	So.	32-0	1.0
11	Malcolm Sims	6-4	Fr.	8-0	1.4

* Cheaney: College Player of Year, Consensus All-America, Big Ten MVP, All-Big Ten, set Big Ten career scoring record (2,613); Graham: All-Big Ten.

Chris Reynolds, at 6-1 not
a frequent flyer above the rim,
celebrates the clinching
of a Big Ten championship.

Big Ten fouls are rarely brushes, as Minnesota's Voshon Lenard demonstrates against Greg Graham.

It was Feb. 22 when Scott May broke an arm at Purdue and the 1975 national championship may have disappeared; Feb. 20, 1977, when one of the best of Knight's Hoosiers, two-year All-American Kent Benson, saw his college career end when his back gave way at Purdue; Feb. 24, 1983, when a team that had been No. 1-ranked lost shooter and leader Ted Kitchel to a back injury at Michigan. And now this, on Feb. 19, to the biggest and youngest player on the country's best team.

Henderson had been a major contributor to a great Hoosier run.

It began with a four-game charge to the Pre-Season NIT championship. The Hoosiers' overtime victory over Florida State in the semifinals Thanksgiving Eve included the Pat Graham foot injury. In the finals, Seton Hall went down battling, 78-74, in about as good a game as college basketball ever has seen in November. That night, in Madison Square Garden and on national TV, Calbert Cheaney scored a career-high 36 points and took

the first long step toward the award he was to receive at season's end: College Player of the Year.

A couple of close ones got away – to Kansas 74-69 at the Hoosier Dome and to Kentucky 81-78 at Freedom Hall – but nobody in the country was playing better basketball as the Hoosiers broke out of the Big Ten gate with 12 straight victories. The scariest was Indiana's first trip to Penn State. The Lions were 1-7 in their first Big Ten season but they led No. 1-ranked Indiana 68-66 with 24.7 seconds to go when they tried to beat Indiana's press with a long, high pass. Greg Bartram caught the ball over Hoosier Chris Reynolds and drove to a layup, but official Sam Lickliter called what he saw: Bartram pushing Reynolds away when both were in the air. What Lickliter, downcourt, looking straight back into the play, didn't see that ESPN's cameras did was Reynolds, beaten on the play, grabbing – fouling – Bartram before they went up. Two free throws by Greg Graham tied the game, and in the second overtime, freshman Brian Evans scored from the baseline with seven seconds left and Indiana came out with an 88-84 escape.

The Hoosiers went from there to a 93-92 Assembly Hall victory over Michigan's "Fab Five." That went alongside a 76-75 victory at Ann Arbor, where Henderson swatted away Chris Webber's attempted follow-in basket just ahead of the buzzer. Michigan had led the second game 70-61 with 11½ minutes to go, but the outcome really wasn't as shaky as the first game. Webber's 30-foot 3-pointer at the buzzer tightened things after Evans had clinched victory by hitting two free throws at 0:02.

That game made Indiana 10-0, No. 5-ranked Michigan 8-3 and effectively ended the championship race.

Until Feb. 19. The Henderson injury's effect on the Hoosier inside game and the player rotation Knight had evolved over the season was a primary uncertainty when Purdue game time came.

Knight's first response was to replace big with little – in effect, a three-guard lineup again with Bailey, Greg Graham and Reynolds along with Cheaney and Matt Nover. Purdue came in with the league's best newcomer: Glenn Robinson, who had 22 points and 10 rebounds when Indiana with Henderson beat the Boilermakers at Mackey Arena, 74-65. This time Robinson had 24 points and 14 rebounds; the other Purdue forward, Cuonzo Martin, had his biggest game of the year, 32 points.

But the matchup at the other end of the court worked to Indiana's favor. The retooled lineup emphasized perimeter play and put three standout 3-point shooters on the floor: Cheaney, Bailey and Greg Graham. It also

Indiana-Louisville wasn't the only squareoff in Regional play at St. Louis, and this one cost both Louisville's Dwayne Morton and Indiana's Calbert Cheaney a technical foul.

gave Graham driving room. No one in Big Ten history ever capitalized better on that. Graham set a league record by hitting 26 of 28 free throws, scoring a career-high 32 although he managed just two field goals, each of them a 3-pointer.

The Hoosiers had one day to refocus from Purdue to a Tuesday night ESPN game at Ohio State. It didn't appear particularly dangerous; Ohio State was 5-8 in the league. But the Buckeyes, down 51-38 early in the second half, won in overtime, 81-77.

The 13-game Indiana winning streak was over. Ideas of an 18-0 league season, achieved by only the 1975 and '76 powerhouses at Indiana, were over. So were thoughts of a decided race.

Indiana went to Minnesota that weekend, aware that another loss – in an arena where the Gophers were 13-1 – would throw the championship race wide open.

Knight inserted 6-8 rookie Evans in Henderson's spot against a big Minnesota front line, and Pat Graham, 6-5, made his first start at guard. Cheaney drew his second foul on a 3-point play that put Minnesota up 29-23 when he was lifted. For the most part, it was backups who pulled the Hoosiers even at halftime, 39-39.

"The team that drew us back to a tie did an excellent job," Cheaney said. "We (starters) made a vow to ourselves just to go out and play our behinds off."

In 3½ minutes, the Hoosiers used an 11-0 spurt to go up 50-39 and take the game under control. Weeks later, Knight called the 86-75 victory "one of the really memorable efforts that I've ever had a team give."

The league race back in hand, the Hoosiers were quick and loose down the stretch. Cheaney entered the Northwestern game at Assembly Hall five points short of Alford's career scoring record, nine short of the Big Ten record. Forty seconds into the game, he had caught Alford – on a baseline jump shot off the opening tip and

A big-moment hug in a big year
for Alan Henderson, Calbert

Cheaney and Damon Bailey.

a quick 3 on the Hoosiers' second possession. He scored his Assembly Hall high, 35, and with 4:13 left in the 98-69 victory that officially clinched a clear-cut Big Ten championship, something unparalleled in the Knight years happened: play stopped to recognize an individual achievement. At a timeout, Cheaney was called to center-court and official Ed Hightower presented him the game ball.

Knight called the Big Ten record "an absolutely outstanding honor for a great kid. The key for anything we've ever done here has been teamwork. I'm often asked why we don't put the names of players on the backs of shirts. I've always felt it was Indiana that was playing, and I always will feel that way. Yet, over the span of time that I've been here, we've had some really outstanding things – where they have been recognized as individuals, but they have accomplished these individual honors through a hell of a cooperative effort."

On Senior Night, the Hoosiers blasted Michigan State, 99-68, then an 87-80 victory at Wisconsin closed out a 17-1 record that lifted the team above every other team that had won a Big Ten championship over an 18-game route except three others from Indiana: the 1952-53 Branch McCracken team that won the national championship (17-1), the 1974-75 team that Knight considers his best (18-0), and the 1975-76 team that remains college basketball's last unbeaten champion (18-0).

The Hoosiers went into the tournament with their confidence as re-established as it could have been, without Henderson. The three-guard lineup had established its own characteristics, primarily quickness and exceptional ability to capitalize on the 3-point shot – 22 points a game from there after Henderson went out, 15.8 before. The change moved Greg Graham forward as a scoring leader. Until Henderson's injury, Graham had just one 25-point game in his career. He averaged 25.0 over the last six regular-season games. He became the

first player to lead the league in both shooting and 3-point shooting, and he became a first-team All-Big Ten player and first-round NBA draftee. He (577 points) and Cheaney (a school-record 785) were the highest scoring duo in IU history with their 1,362 points.

When Cheaney scored 32, Graham 22, and the Hoosiers rolled by strong Louisville, 82-69, in a third-round NCAA tournament game, Indiana had the appearance of a rebuilt team that was as good as before Henderson's injury. Like 1975, when the Hoosiers sailed on unbeaten after losing Scott May, and 1983, when they played some of their best basketball in winning the Big Ten championship after losing Kitchel, the appearance was illusory. The injury loss inevitably showed up.

For the '93 Hoosiers, that moment came against tall Kansas when, minus Henderson, they couldn't combat a high-low combination of 6-10 Eric Pauley and 6-7 Richard Scott (29 combined points, with another 6 from 7-foot Greg Oostertag). "They really only had one true inside guy," Pauley said. "I'd get the ball inside and look for Richard." Indiana led as late as 50-48 but a 10-point Jayhawk burst right there keyed an 83-77 Kansas victory, in old St. Louis Arena, where the first of Knight's Indiana tournament teams had made a valiant try against Bill Walton and UCLA 20 years before.

That one started things. This one ended an era. Seniors Cheaney, Greg and Pat Graham, Nover and Reynolds went out with a three-year Big Ten log of 46-8, bettered over the last 60 years by only the Indiana teams of 1974-76 (48-2) and the Ohio State teams of 1960-62 (40-2). Knight coached the two Indiana teams and played on the Ohio State teams. "I'm incredibly pleased to have had a chance to coach these kids," Knight said hoarsely at St. Louis. "They played themselves into a spot that really will be a great thing in the history of Indiana basketball."

1992 – 1993		
31-4; Big Ten 17-1, Champion		
Murray State [1]	W	103-80
Tulane [1]	W	102-92
Florida State [2]	*W	81-78
Seton Hall [2]	W	78-74
Kansas [3]	L	69-74
at Notre Dame	W	75-70
Austin Peay [4]	W	107-61
Western Michigan [4]	W	97-58
Cincinnati	W	79-64
St. John's	W	105-80
Butler [5]	W	90-48
Colorado [5]	W	85-65
Kentucky [6]	L	78-81
Iowa	W	75-67
Penn State	W	105-57
at Michigan	W	76-75
at Illinois	W	83-79
at Purdue	W	74-65
Ohio State	W	96-69
Minnesota	W	61-57
at Northwestern	W	93-71
at Iowa	W	73-66
at Penn State	**W	88-84
Michigan	W	93-92
Illinois	W	93-72
Purdue	W	93-78
at Ohio State	*L	77-81
at Minnesota	W	86-75
Northwestern	W	98-69
Michigan State	W	99-68
at Wisconsin	W	87-80
N C A A		
Wright State [3]	W	97-54
Xavier [3]	W	73-70
Louisville [7]	W	82-69
Kansas [7]	L	77-83

* *Overtime*
** *Double Overtime*
[1] *Pre-Season NIT, Assembly Hall*
[2] *Pre-Season NIT, New York*
[3] *at Hoosier Dome*
[4] *Indiana Classic*
[5] *Hoosier Classic, Indianapolis*
[6] *at Louisville, Kentucky*
[7] *at St. Louis, Missouri*

Indiana 96   Kentucky 84
Hoosier Dome   Indianapolis, Indiana
December 4, 1993

W hen Damon Bailey opened pre-season practice his senior year at Indiana, there were overtones of Kent Benson and 1977. Like Benson then, Bailey had seen his three-year partners in a great Hoosier basketball era graduate. Unlike Benson, he had one major contributor back from the No. 1-ranked team of the year before: Alan Henderson, now a junior, now moving well on his surgically repaired knee. He also had fellow seniors Pat Graham and Todd Leary.

No.		Height	Class	G-S	Pts.
44	Alan Henderson	6-9	Jr.	30-29	17.8
34	Brian Evans	6-8	So.	27-24	11.9
50	Todd Lindeman	7-0	So.	29-18	5.6
22	Damon Bailey*	6-3	Sr.	30-30	19.6
33	Pat Graham	6-5	Sr.	28-15	11.8
30	Todd Leary	6-3	Sr.	28-12	8.3
23	Steve Hart	6-3	Fr.	30-5	3.9
20	Sherron Wilkerson	6-4	Fr.	28-12	3.2
21	Richard Mandeville	7-0	Fr.	24-3	1.1
25	Pat Knight	6-6	Jr.	27-2	0.7
53	Ross Hales	6-6	Sr.	13-0	0.3

All-Big Ten

But the leadership role that had been chiefly Calbert Cheaney's clearly fell to Bailey, who had been leading basketball teams all his life – three different AAU teams that won national championships with him as MVP during his growing-up years; four Bedford North Lawrence teams that went 99-9, reached the Final Four three times and, climactically, almost mythologically, won the state championship in 1990, his senior year.

Now, it was a different senior year, and it began in the same city where he won that state championship. And it began with the opposite in emotions and experiences: a shocking 75-71 loss to Butler at hallowed Hinkle Fieldhouse. Next up for the team that had just lost to Butler was Kentucky, the No. 1-ranked team in the land.

And this one also was back in Indianapolis, this time at the very scene of Bailey's step into history: the Hoosier Dome. On national TV.

They split the tickets evenly in this annual border battle, whether the game is at The Dome or at

(Left) Bob Knight is a spectator as officials Tom Rucker, Ted Valentine debate.

(Right) Freshman Steve Hart works for leverage against Minnesota's Voshon Lenard.

(Far right) Alan Henderson finds a close-range opening against Boston College and Bill Curley.

21-9; Big Ten 12-6, Third		
at Butler	L	71-75
Kentucky [1]	W	96-84
Notre Dame	W	101-82
Tennessee Tech [2]	W	117-73
Washington State [2]	W	79-64
Eastern Kentucky	W	91-80
at Kansas	*L	83-86
TCU [3]	W	81-65
Western Kentucky [3]	W	65-55
Penn State	W	80-72
at Iowa	W	89-75
Michigan	W	82-72
at Purdue	*L	76-83
Northwestern	W	81-76
Minnesota	W	78-66
at Illinois	L	81-88
Ohio State	*W	87-83
at Penn State	W	76-66
at Michigan	L	67-91
Iowa	W	93-91
Purdue	W	82-80
at Northwestern	W	81-74
at Minnesota	L	56-106
Illinois	W	82-77
at Ohio State	L	78-82
at Michigan State	L	78-94
Wisconsin	W	78-65

N	C	A	A
Ohio [4]		W	84-72
Temple [4]		W	67-58
Boston College [5]		L	68-77

*Overtime
[1] at RCA Dome
[2] Indiana Classic
[3] Hoosier Classic, Indianapolis
[4] at Landover, Maryland
[5] at Miami, Florida

Damon Bailey's senior season had a dazzling December, starting against Kentucky.

Louisville's Freedom Hall. The red-wearing half of the 38,197 at this renewal came into the building with considerably less bloodlust and gusto than the blues.

Hoosier coach Bob Knight added to their unease. After a week of intense practice, neither Henderson nor seniors Graham and Leary started - freshmen Sherron Wilkerson and Steve Hart and sophomores Brian Evans and Todd Lindeman in there with Bailey.

The difference in the two Indiana performances, against Butler and Kentucky, was apparent immediately. Poised, experienced, No. 1-ranked Kentucky committed turnovers on four of its first five possessions. On the sidelines, Knight was as aggressive as his defenders, exhorting and cheering. "That's about as excited as I've been about basketball in a long time," he said, "the way we got started. I kinda became a fan for the first five or six minutes, because I thought we really did play hard."

The payoff was a 6-0 start that became 17-10. Kentucky fired back and when its lead was 33-26 with 7½ minutes left in the half, No. 1 seemed to be asserting itself.

Those last 7½ minutes of the first half, Knight was to marvel later, "We played about as well as I think you could play."

Bailey was the focal point. His second foul came with 4:58 to go in the half, but with Kentucky up 37-35, he stayed in. It was 38-38 when he drove the baseline to a reverse layup, and he made Indiana's lead 43-38 a half-minute later with a 3. In the last two minutes, he drove twice and drew two-shot fouls he converted, and a third time he made the shot as he was fouled, for

a 3-point play. He had 13 of the 29 Indiana points in that closing 7½ minutes and the Hoosiers left the stage to a red roar, up by a stunning 55-44.

Evans hit four field goals in the first four minutes of the second half as the lead widened to 65-50. Travis Ford led a 13-1 Kentucky bolt that tightened things to 66-63 with 12:37 still to play.

Now it was Henderson's turn: a dunk, a press-beating layup, another layup off Leary's lob pass, then two free throws, then an offensive rebound and dunk. With nine minutes still to go, he had put Indiana up 77-68. It was 82-77, when Bailey hit six free throws to close out his 29-point game (16-for-19 on free throws) and a 96-84 Hoosier victory.

"We won the game and we played hard," Bailey said. "That's all we were really worried about. We weren't worried about stopping Travis Ford or stopping Rodrick Rhodes, we were worried about Damon Bailey playing hard and Todd Leary playing hard and just everybody playing hard – getting an Indiana team that's fun to watch again."

Bailey worked at maintaining that, and the Hoosier winning streak reached five. When it ended, it was in a marvelous 86-83 overtime victory for Kansas at Lawrence, a game decided by freshman Jacque Vaughn's 3-point shot at the buzzer and sustained by Bailey's all-out, 36-point effort. "He was sensational," Kansas coach Roy Williams said. "His freshman year at Charlotte (when Kansas ousted the Hoosiers from the 1991 NCAA tournament), he probably played better against us than anybody else. I'm glad the sucker's graduating." Knight said Bailey "played really hard, moved well, worked really well to get the basketball. It was a carry-over of the way he has played all year long."

Bailey went on to an MVP year, an All-Big Ten year, a second-team All-America year. But all those years of basketball seemed to take a physical toll. The summer

after this senior year ended, while he was under contract to the Indiana Pacers who had made him a second-round draft pick, he underwent surgery on both knees. He also had a hip pointer, then played out the last weeks of the season with a torn rib.

The Hoosiers faded from the race in the last two weeks and finished third.

Henderson, who had a 41-point game the last week of the season at Michigan State, scored 34 when the Hoosiers opened their NCAA tournament bid with an 84-72 win over Ohio. Against Temple and the zone defenses that have made John Chaney's team a consistent national power, Knight spread around the perimeter the shooters who made Indiana the national 3-point leader that season. In a 67-58 victory, 3-point shooting by Evans (4-for-6), Leary (3-for-5), Graham (2-for-3) and Bailey (1-for-3) supplied almost half the Hoosier points.

The 21-9 season ended, ironically, against a three-guard team: Boston College, which out-3-pointed the Hoosiers, 10-6, and won, 77-68. Indiana – in the Sweet 16 for a fourth straight time, longest such string in the country – had gone into the last seven minutes ahead, 64-59.

135

(Above right) Bob Knight, always pulling hard.

(Right) Alan Henderson (44) provides some experienced counsel for Todd Lindeman.

Indiana 80   Kansas 61

Assembly Hall

December 17, 1994

Bob Knight shares a laugh at an NCAA tournament press conference.

Freshmen in batches have been keys to big, big years over the Bob Knight seasons at Indiana. But not necessarily – indeed, rarely – in the year the freshmen arrived.

The freshman class of 1972-73 (Scott May, Quinn Buckner, Bobby Wilkerson, Tom Abernethy, Jim Crews) is a candidate for any all-time best list, because of its team accomplishments and the fact that May, Buckner and Wilkerson went in the top 11 of the NBA draft, still the highest ever for three teammates. The freshman class of 1976-77 had injuries and dropouts but still was the nucleus of a team that was No. 1 in the senior year of survivors Mike Woodson and Butch Carter, till more injuries hit. The freshman class of Isiah Thomas in 1979-80 was in on three Big Ten championships and one NCAA, despite losing Thomas halfway through. The freshman class of Steve Alford took some hits along the way but wound up as 1987 NCAA champion. And the freshman class of 1989-90 aged under fire in an 8-10 conference baptism, then put together one of the very best three-year records in Big Ten history.

Senior Alan Henderson and junior Brian Evans,

each with a history of time-costing injuries that required surgery but a future that included No. 1 NBA draft status, were there to check in a new wave of Indiana freshmen this year.

Forward Andrae Patterson had been Player of the Year in Texas; guard Neil Reed, in Louisiana; forward Charlie Miller, in Florida. Michael Hermon was a late addition, his credentials scarred scholastically but as

No.		Height	Class	G-S	Pts.
44	Alan Henderson*	6-9	Sr.	31-31	23.5
34	Brian Evans	6-8	Jr.	31-30	17.4
45	Andrae Patterson	6-8	Fr.	28-20	7.3
5	Neil Reed	6-2	Fr.	30-18	5.9
30	Michael Hermon	6-3	Fr.	28-17	6.0
3	Charlie Miller	6-7	Fr.	31-12	5.6
50	Todd Lindeman	7-0	Jr.	30-10	4.9
23	Steve Hart	6-3	So.	30-14	4.7
25	Pat Knight	6-6	Sr.	31-3	1.5
32	Robbie Eggers	6-10	Fr.	24-0	0.6
4	Jean Paul	6-2	Fr.	10-0	0.8

* All-Big Ten

Alan Henderson's 23.52 scoring average as a senior was No. 1 in Bob Knight's first 25 Indiana years, and Henderson also left with IU's career rebounding record.

strong as the others' on-court.

Henderson, Evans and Knight's son, Patrick, the Hoosier Hoosiers in the group, were given the dual roles of leaders and conveyors of just what that Indiana across the jersey front means — and brings from opponents.

The rookies got an idea of the latter quickly. Their 2-4 start was the worst a Knight team ever had, at that point of the season.

The fourth loss carried some honor with it. At Louisville against the withering Kentucky press, rookie Reed did a remarkable job: 40 minutes, 17 points, 3 turnovers, 3 assists.

But there was, in all that, a fatal freshman flaw. After Reed had beaten the press one more time for a layup that put Indiana ahead 64-62 with 4½ minutes left, his momentum carried him off the court and beyond the end line. On his return, with Kentucky guard Anthony Epps about to throw the ball in-bounds, Reed — still out of bounds — reached out as he ran by Epps and flipped the ball into the air.

Technical foul. Kentucky used it to tie the game with two free throws by Epps and go ahead on two more by Walter McCarty, a one-time Calbert Cheaney teammate at Evansville Harrison. The 'Cats won, 73-70.

Solid victories in the Indiana Classic sent the Hoosiers into semester exams with a 4-4 record. Waiting at the end of them was the stiffest test of all: No. 3-ranked Kansas, the perennial power that in the Roy Williams years had made a specialty of beating good Indiana teams.

This one figured to be one-sided. It was. Unimaginably so.

Patterson, at 6-8 going against 7-foot Greg Oostertag and 6-11 Raef LaFrentz, dominated the Kansas offensive backboard early. In the first seven minutes, he had seven rebounds, six of them at the Kansas end. With Assembly Hall aroar, Indiana's lead opened to 22-12.

It was 27-19 when Oostertag missed a jump shot, Patterson claimed the long rebound and hustling Jerod Haase dived to contest the rebound. Haase crashed into Patterson, who crumpled on the floor, out for the rest of this day (and the next three games) with a "fairly substantial" knee sprain.

There still was a game to play, and the Kansas front line still was huge.

Rather than blunting the Indiana charge, the Patterson injury seemed to work as a stimulant. Indiana put together a 15-0 blitz that put Kansas down 39-19. Indiana got the ball back with 25 seconds left in the half,

(Top) For Brian Evans, a loose ball is a prize worth diving for.

(Left) Basketball is BIG at Indiana.

up 45-25, and 8-year-olds watching across Hoosierland knew what Bob Knight teachings dictated: hold the ball for a last shot.

Freshmen don't always see things like clocks. Reed bolted down the right side and – from even a few feet behind the stripe – sank another 3. Later, Evans smiled about that one. "I guess Neil never has too much of a conscience," he said. "I don't know if *I* would have shot, but – we got some momentum."

The Hoosiers went to halftime up 48-25 and – on a day when they shot .348, second-lowest of their entire 19-12 season – they routed the No. 3 team in the country, 80-61, with 29 points from Evans, 22 from Henderson and 14 from Reed.

"I think they prematurely buried Indiana and Bobby Knight," Williams said. "The team that I saw today just seemed to be so much more intense, more aggressive. Everything we tried to do they seemed to be there a step ahead of us."

Not a lot of nights the rest of the way were as joyful. On Jan. 24, Michigan came in with just Jimmy King and Ray Jackson left from its "Fab Five" era, came in to The Hall where the Fabs had gone 0-3. Indiana had a 50-game home winning streak, longest in the land,

an IU record, matching the Big Ten record the Ohio State teams of Knight's playing days had put together. Michigan overwhelmed Indiana on the boards, 44-27, and won easily, 65-52.

The Hoosiers closed at home with a 110-79 victory over Iowa. The basket that put them over 100 came when the team's two seniors, Henderson and Knight, attacked two-on-one. Knight lofted a high pass that Henderson caught and rammed home for his 34th and 35 points. And then the seniors came out, Knight to a classic, tearful sidelines hug by his dad and coach.

The coach led off Senior Day with a warm tribute to Henderson, whose 23.52 season scoring average wound up just ahead of May's 23.50 as the best in the Knight years.

"I love Alan Henderson," Knight said. "He's one of my favorite players. (Calbert) Cheaney, (Mike) Woodson, there are a ton of them. But…" The voice cracked. "…Patrick Knight is my all-time favorite Indiana player."

A week later at Boise, Idaho, where the 1992 Hoosiers' Final Four drive had begun, this Hoosier season ended with a 65-60 loss to Missouri, a defeat that echoed into the summer. That's when an NCAA Tournament ruling came down: Indiana was fined $30,000 for Knight's anger and use of two profanities over a postgame press conference misunderstanding.

139

(Above right) At a pre-season Big Ten coaches' meeting, Bob Knight gives retiring Michigan State coach Jud Heathcote a surprise hug.

(Right) Bob Knight's Senior Day hug for his 'all-time favorite Indiana player,' son Pat.

Indiana 72   Penn State 54

Assembly Hall

Februrary 14, 1996

W hen first
mentioned, it didn't seem feasible.

Sure, Indiana has the ultimate in team-oriented
programs. But, after the 24 most dominant years in Big Ten
basketball history, after 11 league championships and eight
Big Ten MVPs and 29 first-team All-Big Ten selections
and 15 different players named 25 times to an All-America
team and 14 first-round NBA draft picks, not to mention
all-time Big Ten scoring leader Calbert Cheaney…

Bob Knight locks in on
Neil Reed, eye-to-eye.

No.		Height	Class	G-S	Pts.
34	Brian Evans*	6-8	Sr.	31-31	21.2
45	Andrae Patterson	6-8	So.	31-29	11.3
50	Todd Lindeman	7-0	Sr.	24-12	9.8
5	Neil Reed	6-2	So.	31-28	10.5
3	Charlie Miller	6-7	So.	31-25	8.2
55	Haris Mujezinovic	6-9	Jr.	30-10	6.5
21	Richard Mandeville	7-0	So.	29-4	2.8
32	Robbie Eggers	6-10	So.	29-3	2.3
4	Chris Rowles	6-1	So.	24-0	1.7
23	Kevin Lemme	5-11	Sr.	16-0	0.7
20	Sherron Wilkerson	6-4	So.	17-13	7.5
42	Lou Moore	6-7	So.	3-0	1.0

* Big Ten MVP, All-Big Ten, Big Ten scoring leader

Brian Evans was the first player from the Bob Knight
years to lead the Big Ten in scoring?

The 6-8 left-hander grew up in Terre Haute fanta-
sizing about himself in an Indiana uniform. As a
9-year-old, he said, he would watch a Hoosier telecast,
then "run out to our driveway and pretend I was Randy
Wittman – I was a *big* fan of Randy Wittman. Or Ted
Kitchel – he was a good foul shooter. I can remember
going to the line and trying to imitate Ted Kitchel."

Ted Kitchel, despite back problems, is No. 18 on
Indiana's all-time scoring list. Wittman is No. 12.

Brian Evans is No. 9. He's on there with five teammates in his Indiana years (Cheaney, No. 1; Alan
Henderson, 5; Damon Bailey, 6; Eric Anderson, 8, and

Andrae Patterson powers his way to an open shot.

141

Brian Evans outreaches Penn State's Danny Earl for a loose ball in the Hoosiers' Assembly Hall victory over the No. 8-ranked Nittany Lions.

Greg Graham, 12). There are six others from the Knight years, 14 of the top 20 from a school that has always attracted shooters.

But Brian Evans was the first of the 14 to lead the Big Ten in scoring.

Evans also was the Big Ten MVP, the only unanimous pick on either the coaches' or the media's All-Big Ten teams, Knight's 15th NBA first-round pick and the only Big Ten player taken in this draft.

What didn't happen was what usually accompanies an MVP selection: a league championship. From the time they scrambled to get by Division II Alaska-Anchorage and then lost their next two games in the Great Alaska Shootout, these Hoosiers struggled.

They wound up as the worst-shooting Knight team (.472) since his very first one (.454). They were one of just seven Knight teams with more turnovers than their opponents. Well into their season, they seemed likely to be the first Knight team to miss out on the NCAA tournament in 11 years.

They weren't the luckiest bunch, either. In February, they had finally seemed to have things together, beating Iowa and Northwestern at Assembly Hall and then putting an exceptional game together to win at Minnesota, 81-66, with 25, 27 and 28 points from Evans during that run.

Then they went to Iowa for a Sunday afternoon game. The Hoosiers' road regimen hasn't changed much since the first Knight year. Practice at home, regular afternoon time, before leaving. Flight by university plane to the site. Dinner at the hotel. Film available to watch after dinner. Maybe one more walk-through to cover what's expected from the opponent. A last chat with Knight, probably around 10. Then, bed.

At Iowa, they were disrupted at 10 by a gas leak in the indoor pool area at their hotel. Four hours later, they moved out to another hotel, across town. And 12 hours after that, they took a 76-50 thumping.

Back home, the adversity kept coming. Flu put Andrae Patterson in the hospital the night before the Hoosiers were to play league leader Penn State. Neil Reed and Todd Lindeman also were hit.

Patterson made it to the game and started but played just eight minutes. Reed played the full 40 minutes but hit just one of seven shots. He was 0-for-3 and the whole Indiana team 0-for-11 on 3-point shots, the first time in nine years Indiana didn't hit at least one 3 in a Big Ten game.

Brian Evans' dream of playing in an Indiana uniform ended with his being Bob Knight's first Big Ten scoring champion, and the Big Ten MVP.

1 9 9 5 – 1 9 9 6

19-12; Big Ten 12-6, Second

at Alaska-Anch. [1]	W	84-79
Duke [1]	L	64-70
Connecticut [1]	L	52-86
Notre Dame	W	73-53
Kentucky [2]	L	82-89
Delaware [3]	W	85-68
Bowling Green [3]	W	78-67
Kansas [4]	L	83-91
at Evansville	W	76-48
DePaul	L	82-84
Appalachian State [5]	W	103-59
Weber State [5]	W	82-62
at Michigan State	L	60-65
Ohio State	W	89-67
Wisconsin	W	81-55
at Illinois	W	85-71
at Purdue	L	69-74
Michigan	W	99-83
at Penn State	L	68-82
Iowa	W	76-73
Northwestern	W	95-61
at Minnesota	W	81-66
at Iowa	L	50-76
Penn State	W	72-54
at Michigan	L	75-80
Purdue	L	72-74
Illinois	W	76-64
at Wisconsin	W	76-68
at Ohio State	W	73-56
Michigan State	W	57-53
N C A A		
Boston College [6]	L	51-64

[1] *Alaska Shootout, Anchorage*
[2] *at RCA Dome*
[3] *Indiana Classic*
[4] *at Kansas City, Missouri*
[5] *Hoosier Classic, Indianapolis*
[6] *at Orlando, Florida*

Late in the first half, the Hoosiers seemed to be fading. An 18-15 Indiana lead changed to a 31-24 deficit. But Lindeman, flu and all, was playing well. His rebound basket, part of a 12-point, 11-rebound night, came just ahead of the buzzer and gave Indiana a 36–35 halftime lead.

Indiana led 62-54 when Evans drove the baseline and slammed the ball through with a reverse, two-handed dunk. The Hoosiers sailed from there to a 72-54 wipeout of a team that had come in 17-2 and ranked No. 8 in the nation – an all-new basketball experience for Happy Valley. The Lions became the 14th straight nationally ranked team to lose in The Hall.

"Brian Evans all year has just been a giant for this team," first-year coach Jerry Dunn said.

The Indiana victory moved Hoosier rival Purdue into the league lead, on the brink of pulling away to its third straight league championship. It got there, in part by ending that string of Assembly Hall losses by ranked teams. Purdue came in No. 5 and won, 74-72.

At that point, Indiana was 15-11 and 8-6 in the league, its tourney status questionable. The rest of the way, the Hoosiers had two seniors leading them – not just Evans but also Lindeman, who put the best games of his career together when it was closing out. Lindeman had 21 in the Purdue game, 19 in a win at Wisconsin, a career-high 28 for a victory at Ohio State, and 15 (with Evans' 23) in a Senior Day win over Michigan State that lifted the Hoosiers to a 12-6 league finish and a share of second place.

One more time, their tournament run stopped before it got started. Boston College scored the last 10 points to win, 64-51, in a first-round game at Orlando. Evans, swarmed over all night by Boston College defenders, hit just 2 of 14 shots and scored 7 points in a disappointing career finish that had its irony. Three months later, it was the team that plays in the arena where that happened, Orlando, that made Evans its first-round draft pick.

USA 8-0
Los Angeles, California
Summer 1984

So much had gone into the two-year leadup that Bob Knight, not a person easily thrilled, admitted he was – on opening day of his United States team's 1984 Olympic quest at Los Angeles.

It was a Sunday afternoon, and the 12 American Olympian basketball players ran onto the Forum court for pregame warmups. They burst onto the stage before a full house, and ignited a roar.

The immediate followup was a chant loud and throaty: "USA! USA! USA!"

Team manager C. M. Newton and head coach Bob Knight saw little to correct in the U.S. team's gold-medal run at Los Angeles.

"When I heard that, it was kind of a hair-raising experience for me," Knight said. "I was very pleased that the players were able to enjoy something like that."

It touched all the emotional chords that Knight had spent the summer trying to reach with the players who emerged as America's select team. They had started as 74, who responded to invitations sent out just after the Final Four in Seattle that year. Competition in Bloomington cut the field to 32, then to 20. From that group, 16 came back for the final preparations, and 12 emerged.

And when he first met with the select 12, he told them: "There has to be a rapport between coaches and players – a feeling for one another, a combined effort toward an eventual goal that on the night of Aug. 10 each one of you 12 will be standing on a platform, with the national anthem being played, and a gold medal around your neck.

"That's what this is all about."

No.		Height	Weight	G-S	Pts.
9	Michael Jordan	6-5	199	8-8	17.1
13	Chris Mullin	6-6	211	8-1	11.6
6	Patrick Ewing	7-0	248	8-6	11.0
4	Steve Alford	6-1	163	8-4	10.3
12	Wayman Tisdale	6-9	259	8-2	8.6
14	Sam Perkins	6-9	233	8-8	8.1
8	Alvin Robertson	6-4	193	8-5	7.8
7	Vern Fleming	6-5	184	8-4	7.7
5	Leon Wood	6-3	190	8-2	5.9
10	Joe Kleine	6-11	269	8-0	3.4
11	Jon Koncak	7-0	250	8-0	3.3
15	Jeff Turner	6-9	229	8-0	1.6

144

Indiana's Steve Alford, the youngest 1984 U.S. Olympian, won a starting spot, shot .644 and 'carried his weight,' in the eyes of his Olympic and Hoosier coach, Bob Knight.

Henry Iba, who coached three U.S. Olympic teams, was Bob Knight's choice to be part of the 1984 coaching staff, and to be the first coach carried off the floor on the shoulders of the gold-medal U.S. team.

Knight gave every player a 3x5 photograph of an Olympic gold medal. "I told them 'I want this in your pocket, whatever you have on, wherever you go, until the real thing is yours.'"

Before the 32 were cut down, all played in two doubleheaders that packed Assembly Hall. An all-IU group, stretching from the Van Arsdale Twins (senior year 1965) through a Hoosier with eligibility left, 1985 graduate Uwe Blab of the West German Olympic team, played the Olympians before 17,113 at Assembly Hall on June 22. It amounted to a final exam before the last cutdown from 16. The Olympians won, 124-89, with 16 points and 7-for-7 shooting by Jordan.

And then there were 12 – a team that Knight took across the country. Every place it stopped, it drew huge crowds. And it won, against professional all-star teams that volunteered to give the Olympians a valid checkout before their Olympic test. The biggest of those games was back home in Indiana, where a crowd that still is the record for basketball in the United States, 67,596, turned out on July 9 for the first event at the brand new Hoosier Dome in Indianapolis. The Olympians won, 97-82, over an NBA team that included home-stater Larry Bird (14 points in 26 minutes), Isiah Thomas (10 points, 7 assists and 4 steals in 23 minutes) and others, including three more ex-Hoosiers: Mike Woodson, Quinn Buckner and Randy Wittman.

The team's last pre-Los Angeles training stop was in San Diego. There, Knight brought out a guest. Probably

there wasn't a U.S. player who knew of the basketball greatness of Alex Groza, from Kentucky's 1948 and '49 NCAA champions, and America's 1948 Olympic gold-medal team. Probably none knew, either, of the tragic side of the Groza career: the point-shaving scandals that surfaced in 1951 and got Groza, by then not just an NBA star but also a part-owner of his Indianapolis Olympians team, a lifetime ban from the sport.

"Alex was living in San Diego, and he and (Knight's Olympic assistant) C.M. Newton had played together in college. I had Alex come to practice one morning, and bring his gold medal along.

"He had made it into a necklace for his wife. Alex passed that gold medal around to our players, and each kid looked at it, and each kid thought about what he was going to do with his gold medal. I could just see it in their faces: each kid held it, and each kid was reluctant to pass it on to the next kid, till all 12 of them had held that gold medal.

"When they gave it back to Alex, I said: 'How many of you have a thought as to what you want to do with your gold medal, and to whom you want to give it?'

"Each kid kinda smiled. And each kid raised his hand."

It happened. The night of Aug. 10, the Americans whipped Spain, 96-65, and the golds were theirs.

These were the last American collegians to go for gold and get it. They formed a team that went alongside Pete Newell's 1960 gold medalists as maybe the best amateur teams ever. The 1960 team included Oscar

Robertson and Jerry West. The 1984 team had Michael Jordan, plus Patrick Ewing.

It also had Steve Alford, Hoosier.

Alford was the only college freshman on the team. He was there out of concern for the zone defenses most international teams play. Alford and Chris Mullin of St. John's were the acknowledged shooters on the team, and they lived up to the role. Alford ultimately played his way into a starting spot – with Jordan, Ewing, Sam Perkins of North Carolina and Alvin Robertson of Arkansas. Alford was 5-for-6 with 10 points and seven assists in 27 minutes the gold medal game. In the

Olympians' eight Los Angeles games, designated zone-buster Alford shot .644. "Alford," Knight said proudly afterward, "carried his weight."

Canada coach Jack Donohue, Kareem Abdul-Jabbar's high school coach at New York's Power Memorial when Kareem was Lew Alcindor, coached his team into the medal round and lost to the U.S. in the semifinals, 78-59. After the game, he mused out loud:

"Are there a lot of coaches who could take this team and win a gold medal?

"Yes.

"Are there a lot of coaches who could make them play like this?

"No. There's only one Bobby Knight."

Others on the team were Wayman Tisdale of Oklahoma, Vern Fleming of Georgia, Leon Wood of Fullerton State, Jon Koncak of Southern Methodist, Jeff Turner of Vanderbilt and Joe Kleine of Notre Dame.

147

Patrick Ewing was one of the future Hall of Famers who blended together into the gold-medal U.S. team at Los Angeles.

ACKNOWLEDGMENTS

Bob Hammel

Sports editor of the Bloomington Herald-Times for 30 years, Bob Hammel wrote six previous books, five on Indiana basketball. Selected by his peers as Indiana Sportswriter of the Year 17 times, he has been president of the U.S. Basketball Writers Assn., the Football Writers Assn. of America, and the National Sportscasters and Sportswriters Assn.

Hammel, who attended Indiana University, had a 42-year career in Indiana sportswriting, starting with nine years at his hometown newspaper, the Huntington Herald-Press. He also was with the Peru Daily Tribune, Fort Wayne News-Sentinel, Kokomo Morning Times and Indianapolis News before going to Bloomington in 1966. For The Herald-Times, he covered Indiana sports, many national sports events, and five Olympics.

He received the National Basketball Hall of Fame's Curt Gowdy Award (1995), the Silver Medal of the Indiana Basketball Hall of Fame (1996), the Jake Ward Award of the College Sports Information Directors Assn. (1996) and the Bert McGrane Award of the Football Writers Assn. of America (1996).

He retired as sports editor and columnist of the Herald-Times following the 1996 Olympics. He and his wife Julie live in Bloomington and have two children and two granddaughters.

Rich Clarkson

Currently the owner of a publishing and photographic company in Denver, Colo., Rich Clarkson has served as director of photography of The National Geographic Society, as an assistant managing editor of The Denver Post, and, for 20 years, as director of photography of The Topeka (Kansas) Capital-Journal. He has been a contract photographer for Sports Illustrated for 25 years and he still contributes to the magazine.

His company manages all photography for the National Collegiate Athletic Assn., and he helped create the NCAA Hall of Champions museum at its Kansas City headquarters. Clarkson's company also manages photography and publishing for several professional teams, including the Colorado Rockies baseball club. Included in its books produced are *Game Day USA,* a look at college football, and *I Dream A World,* portraits of great American black women as photographed by Brian Lanker, a book now in its 15th printing.

Clarkson has photographed events ranging from 40 NCAA Final Four basketball tournaments (the first as a college freshman when his Kansas University team won the championship, and his second when his Kansas team lost in the championship game the next year to Indiana) to eight Olympics. He was manager of all photography in the main Olympic Stadium for the 1996 Atlanta Games.

Clarkson has been president of the National Press Photographers Assn. and a judge of many competitions, including the Pulitzer Prizes, the Sasakawa Foundation awards and "Pictures of the Year." He serves on the boards of several journalism organizations.

Photography Credits

In addition to the photographs of Rich Clarkson, many of which were done initially for Sports Illustrated magazine, most photographs came from the files of the Bloomington Herald-Times. Herald-Times photographers whose work is included are David Snodgress and Larry Crewell, the newspaper's chief photographers during the 25 years, along with staff photographers Phil Whitlow, John Terhune, Russ Cockrum, David Schreiber, David Mather and Kent Phillips.

Additional photographs came from David Repp, page 88; Bob Hammel, pages 16, 90 and 91; Andy Hayt for Sports Illustrated, page 145, and the Associated Press, page 101 right.

148